OBSCURED

The Obscured Series, Book 1

TARA SUE ME
WRITING AS
CAT WATERS

Tara Sue Me
Cat Waters
www.tarasueme.com

Obscured/Tara Sue Me and Cat Waters -- 1st ed.
ISBN 978-0-692-54601-7

To my husband, who had this crazy idea for the book I thought was going to be women's fiction.

Chapter One

The day I meet Isaiah Martin for the second time, I am running late. I pride myself on my punctuality, not to mention that my clients demand it, and I'm not paying attention to my surroundings.

I look at my watch again. *Five minutes after. Shit.* I scurry through the hotel lobby, making a beeline to the elevators. If luck happens to be on my side, I won't have to wait, but the elevators in the largest hotel in Las Vegas are notoriously slow.

Will the stairs be quicker? I glance over my shoulder. The stairwell is located on the other side of the large open atrium. With my client's room on the thirtieth floor, the elevator is faster, even if I have to wait. I turn back to the elevators.

And run right into a man standing in my path, overcorrect, and twist my ankle.

"Excuse me, ma'am," he says in a soft, cultured Southern accent, reaching out a hand to steady me. "You okay?"

"Damn it!" My ankle throbs so much I'm not sure I can walk. I gingerly put my weight on the hurt ankle and curse again at the pain.

Suck it up, Athena. This is nothing. Think about what'll happen if you don't make it upstairs in the next few minutes.

"Ma'am?" Mr. Southern Gentleman repeats.

"I'm fine." I tentatively move my foot side to side. "Just give me a minute."

"Why don't you come sit down and let me take a look at that ankle?"

"You a doctor?" Odds are he's just your standard pervert wanting the chance to run his hand up my leg. Even if he is a doctor, I'm not about to let him put his hands on me. Not a wise thing to do, since it's almost a certainty Mike will find out.

"No, ma'am," he says. "But I think you may need to rest that ankle just a bit."

"Really, I'm fine." I put my full weight on the ankle and nearly fall over as the pain sparks up my leg. "Ow. Ow. Ow. *Hell.*"

He doesn't speak again, but takes me by the arm and leads me to a bench near the elevators. His head drops down and he runs a finger along my anklebone. Pokes and prods me. "I don't think anything's broken, but you should probably stay off your feet for the next little bit."

"Easy for you to say," I snap. "You're obviously not the one running late."

He looks up and our eyes meet.

Warm caramel eyes. His thick, black hair is long overdue for a haircut and curls up the tiniest bit at his neck. His firm lips give way to a perfect "O" of surprise at the exact moment I recognize him.

"Athena?"

"Isaiah?"

He embraces me with a crushing hug. "Imagine seeing you here. How are you?"

My spine goes rigid, and I don't return the hug. "I'm....I'm fine," I stutter while my eyes dart around the lobby, trying to see if anyone's watching me.

"I can't believe it's you." He is oblivious to my discomfort. "Are you in town for long?"

I force myself to stop scanning the area and focus on Isaiah instead. A cold chill runs down my spine as I take in his handsome features. The last twelve years have treated him well. No longer is he the awkward teenage boy plagued by acne and thick glasses. He's grown into the handsome man I always knew lay beneath the surface.

He looks at me in expectation. What did he ask?

I fiddle with the hem of my skirt. It rests just above the knee. "I live here."

"Here in Vegas?"

Not only is my skirt too short, but my shirt shows too much cleavage. I pull the edges, but can't get them to cover me anymore. "Yes, not far from here."

He looks me up and down. "What are you running late for?"

If I was an honest person, I'd tell him. After all, he looks nice enough. A striking combination of scruffy and clean cut that somehow works. But I'm not honest. Let's face it, I get paid for sex.

"Just a party," I lie. "Last one there has to buy the first round."

"I see," he says, and for a brief moment I fear he does.

"It was nice to see you." I grimace at the thought of putting weight on my bad ankle. "Have a good time in Vegas. Don't blow it all in one place."

"I'm actually living here, too."

"You are?" I'd lifted myself part way off the bench, but at his statement, I sit back down. Does that mean I'll run into him? I'm not sure how I feel about that. "What do you do?"

"I'm a pastor."

My laughter draws the glances of several people in the lobby. I laugh so hard I lose my breath. I almost punch his shoulder and say, "Good one" before I realize he isn't laughing. "Oh, shit," I say instead. "You're serious."

He nods.

"Fuck." My hand flies up to cover my mouth. "I mean, oh crap."

Finally, he laughs. "I can promise you my ears are not so delicate that I'll be offended by language."

I notice he didn't say the word, though. "Sorry, I just wasn't expecting you to say that."

"Obviously."

"I really should be going. I have somewhere to be." I look down at my watch and frown. "Ten minutes ago."

"I won't keep you. I just want to make sure your ankle's fine."

"I'm sure it is now." I stand on my good leg and tentatively put a bit of weight on the bad one. "Ow. Damn it." Nope, still hurts like hell. No way am I going anywhere soon.

"Have a seat and tell me what you've been up to. How you—" he waves, the movement encompassing the hotel lobby.

"Came to Vegas?" I finish for him, when what I really should tell him is what I do in Vegas. But again, I'm not honest.

"Yes, that."

"Mama died." I give him a sideways look, keeping my focus on the lobby when I'm not looking at him. "You remember she had cancer?"

"Yes. That's why you moved. So your dad could get her better care."

Our small town had been ill-equipped to handle the terrible progression of mama's illness. I clutch my skirt tight in my hands, still remembering the look on the doctor's face when he told us there was nothing else they could do.

"Something happened to dad after she died," I say. "Something snapped. He took off one day and never came back." I straighten my shoulders. "I was sixteen. I didn't know what to do."

"Wasn't there anyone you could go to?" he asks. "A family member? Someone?"

He speaks in the soft, soothing accent I associate with my childhood. And his voice doesn't hold condemnation or judgement.

"We were in a strange city," I continue. "I didn't know anyone. So much of my time had been spent caring for mama. When dad left, I decided to leave. To buy a bus ticket for Vegas and become a showgirl."

Except I knew nothing about being a showgirl. The ballet classes I'd taken as a child weren't enough to prepare me for the demanding footwork required of a Vegas dancer.

"That didn't work out," I say. "But I liked Vegas. Liked the crowds and the noise and I could put up with the weather. So I stayed." There's not much else to say, not that won't give away my real profession.

An uncomfortable silence follows, and I say the first thing I can think of, "Tell me about this church of yours."

A smile takes over his face. "It hasn't started yet. I was actually here tonight talking to Mike Randolph about it."

Ah, fuck.

I feel clammy and my heart pounds. "Are you on your way to see him?"

"I just left his office," he says, and I breath a small sigh of relief. "Church starts this Sunday in the Playmaker's Lounge."

My head spins and spots dance before my eyes. "Here? That one?" I point down the hall, in the hopes that he's talking about another Playmaker's Lounge.

"That's the one. Sunday at ten. Mike said it wouldn't be a problem as long as we're out by eleven. Real nice guy, Mike."

I'm going to throw up. Not only am I horribly late, but the odds now point to me seeing Isaiah around town. And he thinks Mike is a *nice guy.* I can't deal with this right now. I struggle to my feet and balance precariously on one foot.

"I'm sorry," I say. "It was good to see you, but I'm really late, and I have to go."

The elevator dings as it arrives, and I jump inside and push the button for the thirtieth floor without waiting for him to say goodbye.

Chapter Two

"You're late," Theo, my client, says, pulling me into the room as soon as I knock.

I stumble a bit on my sore ankle and bite the inside of my cheek so I don't scream out in pain. "I'm sorry," I say. "I was —"

"I don't fucking care. You were expected over fifteen minutes ago."

He's dragged me into the sitting area of the suite, and I look around and discover there's another man in the room. He's sitting on the couch, though, so I can't see him very clearly. I swallow. I wasn't expecting anyone other than Theo.

The meeting with Isaiah has stripped me of the carefully constructed mask I hide behind, and I'm surprised at the way my mind rebels at what's been planned for me this evening. I'm not new at this job. I've done the three-way thing before. It's just that talking with Isaiah brought a strange sense of normal to my life. A normal that didn't include providing sex for money. A normal that whispered of years gone by in a soft Southern accent, I'd long ago given up hope of ever hearing again.

I look up to see Theo frowning at me and I realize that normal is a very dangerous thing for me to be.

You aren't normal. You've never been normal. And you never will be normal.

It was a hard truth to accept years ago, and tonight it's even harder. I close my eyes and allow myself a deep breath. I have to get it together, and quickly, or things are going to go very badly for me.

When I open my eyes, I am once more the woman I was before running into Isaiah. I am Athena and I am a prostitute. This is my life, and a coincidental meeting in a hotel lobby hasn't changed that.

Prove it. I whisper to myself in a voice that no longer holds a trace of Southern accent.

I slowly unbutton my shirt. "Fifteen minutes? I'll have to make it up to you."

He's staring at my chest now, his eyes glued to the skin being exposed inch by inch. "Damn straight you will," he says, but his voice has lost that dangerous edge.

I slip deeper inside my head. Into that place that allows my body to do things I wouldn't do if I thought about them too much. That place that's kept me alive for years. I can't afford to stay out of it for very long. It's a luxury that has no place in my world.

"Is your friend not joining us?" I ask. "Is he waiting for an invitation?"

Theo shakes his head as if remembering where he is and calls out, "You're missing our toy for the evening, Harris."

My hands don't want to move anymore. Harris. Dear Lord, not him. Anyone but him. I don't want to be here in front of Harris. I grit my teeth and hope it's a different Harris.

But as the man on the couch gets to his feet and turns around, I see that it is him.

"Athena," he grinds out.

I nod in silent acknowledgement.

Harris is one of Mike's business associates. In another place and another time, I might have found Harris handsome. He's tall and well built, with sandy colored hair and eyes a deep dark blue hue I've never seen anyone else have.

But it's not another place and time. It;s now and it's Vegas, and I can't think of him as handsome. Especially when I know he'll tell Mike about my tardiness. Mike will know. I don't allow myself to think beyond that at the moment.

"Finally want to sample the goods?" I almost purr.

He's looking at me with an unreadable expression, and it confuses me. I'm typically able to read a man's face when he's with me.

"Not particularly." His arms are crossed and he's frowning.

"Come on, Harris," Theo says. "What's your problem?"

"Nothing," Harris replies. "Except maybe I'm not in a mood to be with a woman so many men have already sampled."

Theo laughs. "Could have fooled me. You didn't have any trouble with the set of twins we had two weeks ago. Remember? Come on, you weren't *that* drunk."

Harris stiffens at the reminder of whatever wild times Theo spoke about. "Yes, I remember very well. But this one—" He nods toward me. "Is off limits to me. She's Mike's girl."

"Aw, fuck, man. I forgot." Theo looks me up and down. "Guess that means you'll just have to watch while I enjoy her."

I try not to think about the fact that they're discussing me like I'm not in the room. Like I'm a piece of meat or an animal or something. I find it takes entirely too much brain power and blame that on the meeting with Isaiah.

Please don't let me run into him often.

I know if I see him regularly, that place deep inside me that allows me to do what I do will go away forever.

Something flickers across Harris's face, but I find I am, once again, unable to tell what.

"I don't think so," he says in reply. "I don't get much out of sex when it's a spectator sport."

Theo shrugs. "Suit yourself. You leaving?"

Harris nods. "Yeah. I think I'll go on. You guys have fun."

But I'm slowly unzipping my skirt and Harris is no longer on Theo's mind. The door closes behind Harris. I take another deep breath, and get to work.

I hadn't lied to Isaiah when I told him I tried to be a Vegas dancer. I just didn't tell him the whole truth. I most certainly didn't tell him what happened after the audition.

The audition for the new group of dancers is finally over. I tell myself it's okay and I'll find some way to earn a living. The rumbling of my stomach reminds me it's been too long since my last decent meal and hunger didn't help my audition at all.

I'm in the dressing room, head down, stuffing my leotard and tights into my bag. Around me the other girls are chatting, but I'm not interested in talking. I want to go back to my hotel room and sleep. I try not to think about how close I am to running out of money.

The chatting stops suddenly and I'm aware of a presence beside me. I keep my head down, the shoes go into the bag next.

"Miss Athena."

His voice is soft. Seductive. I look up and recognize one of the men from the audition. He didn't run it, but he was in the room the entire time. Toward the back. Watching. He is breathtakingly handsome and he gives me a smile.

"Yes," I manage to say.

"You're not a dancer."

There is faint giggling from the girls left in the room and my face heats up. "Did you really come back here to tell me that? Seriously?"

"Only because I'm not looking for a dancer."

His comment confuses me and he sees that because a knowing grin spreads across his face, almost as if he knows what I'll say next.

"What are you looking for?" I ask.

"Come have dinner with me and I'll tell you."

My stomach gurgles at the thought of food and his smile grows bigger. I narrow my eyes. "I don't even know your name."

"Mike," he says. "Mike Randolph."

He is charming at dinner, so much so that it doesn't strike me as odd when what he's looking for never comes up. That night, I curl up in bed with a full stomach and a smile and the promise of another date with Mike.

Men come in all shapes and sizes. Everyone knows that, me perhaps more intimately than most. They come in all dispositions, too. Some you figure out as soon as you meet them: the mama's boy, the wannabe jock, the ass-kisser. Some you aren't sure about until later, when you've peeled back the layers of who they portray themselves to be and see who they really are.

And some, by the time you find out what they are, well, it's much too late.

Chapter Three

It's a damn stupid thing I'm getting ready to do. My hand trembles slightly as I slip my blonde hair into a ponytail. I check my makeup for the fifth time in the mirror and twist and turn, so I can check out all sides of me. I have to look perfect. I have to be perfect.

My ankle is still a bit sore when I slide my feet into my heels, but I'm not stupid enough to wear flats.

I leave my tiny apartment near the airport and catch a bus to the high rise building that houses the office I'm visiting. It's midmorning, and a lot of people are still sleeping, the streets nowhere near as crowded as they will be later tonight. I'm thankful for the diversity of the city because no one looks twice at me.

Once off the bus, I stand in front of the large building and look up, telling myself I have to do this. I have to know why. Why him out of all the people in the country? It's that need that moves me forward. The office I'm looking for is on the forty-second floor. I've stepped foot in it exactly twice. If I am fortunate it will be quick. I don't allow myself to think about what will happen if I'm not fortunate.

I probably should have told Isaiah that starting a church in Vegas was a bad idea. Especially in a lounge. This is Vegas: Sin City. No one is interested in attending church.

Cheap prime rib and easy women? Yes.

Church? Not so much.

My breathing is calm by the time the elevator reaches the floor I need. I take a deep breath, and pretending I'm not scared or worried, I open the door that has MIKE RANDOLPH in harsh gold lettering.

I throw a smile I don't feel at his secretary, Cybil. She was here the last two times I came, and she doesn't like me. I don't have a chance to speak before she's looking down her hawkish nose at me.

"Athena." She's not even trying to keep the contempt out of her voice. "I don't see you on Mr. Randolph's schedule this morning."

I play up the Southern accent I can bring out when needed, drawing out my syllables as far as they can go. "Now Cybil, Sugar, Mike always told me to stop by anytime. Why don't you be a dear and see if he'll see me?" I wiggle my fingers at her phone.

Her nostrils flare, but she snatches up the phone and punches two buttons. I give her an exaggerated wink and an air kiss.

"Mr. Randolph." She gives me the evil eye while she talks. "Athena Hamilton's here to see you. She doesn't have an appointment."

There's a pause, and I pretend to examine my nails. It's all an act. I'm fucking scared to death, but damned if I'll let her know.

"Go on in," she finally says.

I'm sure she sees the way my body is trembling as I pass her, and I hate that she probably gets some sort of satisfaction at my fear. To counteract that fear, I don't hesitate as I push the door open and step inside.

His office is cold. That's the first thing I notice. I don't have the opportunity to look around because my attention is drawn to the man standing in the middle of the room, waiting.

He's wearing an Italian suit, and his shoes boast a spotless sheen. He looks like a Greek god: flawless dark hair, gorgeous olive skin, and piercing dark eyes. Every woman's version of Prince Charming is standing before me, but all I see is my worst nightmare.

"Athena, love. It's been too long. What brings you by?" He moves forward to embrace me, and though his words are warm, his voice is not.

I do my best not to flinch at his touch, picking imaginary lint off his coat as a distraction. "I can't stop by just because?"

"Of course you can. I'm only surprised you're up this early."

I normally sleep until noon. Nervous energy woke me today at eight. "Baby," I purr. "You know I have energy to burn."

"Really?" He leans close and his breath is warm against my neck as he whispers, "Would that explain your tardiness last night?"

Harris.

He laughs at the way my body tenses. "You really think I wouldn't hear? Go sit down."

My seat choices are a couch or a delicate modern chair in front of his desk. I head for the chair that looks like the air conditioning should have knocked it over. Mike moves to sit at his desk, and once he's there, he sits and temples his fingers.

"Tell me why you're really here."

There's no use in pretending there's any reason other than the truth. I take a deep breath and try to act like I'm just shooting the breeze. "I ran into Isaiah Martin last night. I know him. From before."

"Oh, dear. I thought I'd taught you. There is no before. And there is no later unless I allow it. You only get now."

Coming today was a very bad mistake, and I look at my hands folded neatly in my lap. I try to think of how to get out of the office.

"Of course, Sir. How silly of me to forget."

"Look at me."

He smiles at the fear I know is in my eyes. "Isaiah Martin is a man of God," he says. "What makes you think he wants anything to do with a whore?"

"I don't think —"

"That's right, you don't. You're good for one thing, and it's not for what's between your ears."

I have one chance, and I take it. "You're right, of course." I start to stand. "I'll just be going."

"Sit. Down."

Chance gone. I sit down and brace for the inevitable. He reaches for the phone, and I try to stop my legs from trembling.

"Cybil," he says into the handset while keeping his eyes on me. "Clear my calendar for the next two hours."

He locks the office door, and my breathing returns to normal.

"You will forget Isaiah Martin."

My mind has shut down by the time he walks to stand in front of me.

"You need a reminder of who you belong to." He unbuttons his shirt with deliberate slowness and takes off his belt. "Move to the couch, Athena."

Chapter Four

It's hard for me to remember much after that. The parts I do recall have nothing to do with Mike, but with a soft voice that's rough around the edges. The owner of the voice lifts me up and when I whimper, he murmurs reassuring things gently into my ear.

I think I make out something that sounds like, "Get you out," and I laugh in my sleep because if there was a way of doing that, I'd have found it by now. But just as I think that, I'm tucked into bed. It feels so good, I want to curl up in the sheets and never leave.

When I wake again, the shadows have grown long, and I hear bits and pieces of a one-sided argument.

"fucking insane.....really necessary? ...didn't file charges."

I almost risk a peek, but I fear making it a reality. It is so much better to imagine the one with the rough voice is Isaiah and he's going to save me. But whoever is on the phone isn't getting very far with his argument. He's sighing and sounds resolved.

Finally he hangs up the phone and his footsteps approach my bed. The fingers that brush my cheek are reverent. "Little longer," he says and is gone.

My body aches all over, and I could weep for the loss of the voice. But I'm too weak to do anything but fall back asleep.

I'm not sure how long I sleep. I wake feeling achy and sore, and I moan.

"Are you awake?"

I remember Isaiah being in my room while I slept. Or at least I thought it was Isaiah. Either way, I'm shocked at the sound of my friend Vicki's voice.

She's peering over me, her long dark hair almost brushing my face. I want to come back with a snarky reply, but when I open my mouth, all that comes out is another moan.

Her perfectly shaped eyebrows furrow. "Someone slipped a note under my door that you needed help. I used my key and oh my God, who did this?"

She's genuinely worried, and that freaks me out a bit because I must look like shit. I need to see what I look like, and I struggle to sit up.

"Let me." Vicki pulls me into a sitting position and passes me a glass of water.

I gulp it down in a matter of seconds, probably not the best decision because I end up choking and almost spew it all out.

"I was going to say small sips, but I guess it's a bit late for that."

I give her a weak smile. "Slightly."

She pours more water and sits on the edge of my bed, watching to make sure I drink this glass slower. We simply sit in silence until I finish and she says one word.

"Mike?"

Vicki is another one of Mike's girls. Originally from New York, she started working for Mike shortly after I did. We'd become close in the last nine years, and her apartment is a few doors down from mine. She has gorgeous long, black hair and is delicately beautiful. But more than that, she's my only friend.

I nod in reply to her question. "It was my fault. I provoked him."

Her sigh is sad. "Girl, you know better. What were you thinking?"

I balance the cup on my knees and run a finger along the rim. "Have I ever told you about Isaiah Martin?"

"Not that I can remember." She reads my mood too well to ask where in the world I'm going with my question.

"Isaiah and I grew up together. He was my first kiss. We were twelve."

"You were twelve when you had your first kiss?" she asks as if I'd told her I'd been born to royalty and lived on the moon for my first three years. "And you ended up here at seventeen?"

"Yes," I say. "It's really not that late you know."

"Sorry. Didn't mean anything by it. Besides." She kicks off her sandals and tucks her legs underneath her. "This, I gotta hear."

"Isaiah's family lived next door to mine," I say. "We grew up together. Our mothers used to get together and joke about how we'd grow up and get married. I guess they just assumed nothing would ever change. Mama wouldn't get cancer and die. Dad wouldn't go off half-crazy and leave me all alone." I shake my head. "But life happens; things do change."

"You gonna spill about the kiss, or not?" she asks. "Because I can do depressing all by myself."

"There's not much to tell. We were twelve and at some middle school dance. A slow song came on and he asked me to dance. I remember his hands were so sweaty. He kept wiping them as he asked me."

"Ah, sweet. Sweat."

I roll my eyes. "Anyway, we were dancing. I don't remember the song."

"Wait," he says, when the song comes to an end. He keeps his hands on my shoulders and looks at me all nervous-like. "I want to kiss you. Can I?"

Tears spring to my eyes at the sweet memory of a boy asking to kiss me. No one asks me if they can do anything anymore.

"I said yes, of course." I blink my eyes to keep the tears at bay. The gym had been all stuffy and sticky and smelled like a hundred nervous preteens. "His lips were chapped. Funny, the things you remember."

"My first kiss was Frankie MacDonald." Vicki squints her eyes. "He was ten. I don't remember his lips."

"I remember Isaiah's." But it's not Isaiah's twelve-year old lips I remember, rather his soft smiling ones from days before. "I don't think they're chapped anymore."

"Whoa! Hold up. What do you mean you don't think they're chapped anymore?" She looks at me closer. "Have you seen his lips recently?"

I notice my hands are shaking. I only hope Vicki doesn't see them, or if she does, that she attributes it to my meeting with Mike.

"Yes," I say. "I saw him the day before yesterday."

"Oh, no. Was he a job?"

My mind spins at the implication I'd ever do that with Isaiah. That Isaiah would ever do that with me. Then I nearly laugh at the fact that I've been a prostitute for nearly ten years and call what I do *that.*

"No," I say. "He wasn't a trick."

"That's a relief. 'Cause that would be really awkward. So, what were you doing looking at Isaiah Martin's lips if he wasn't a job?"

I blow a long stream of air across the top of my water to watch the waves it makes. "He's a preacher. Mike's letting him start a church in Playmakers."

She almost swallows her gum. "You're kidding?"

I smile a bit at catching Vicki off guard. She normally hears all the gossip before I do.

"Would I kid about something like that?" I ask.

"No," she finally agrees. "I don't think you would."

"Isaiah's starting a church," I explain. "He said Mike was a really nice guy. I went up to Mike's office to ask him about it and, well, here I am."

"That was your first mistake. Going up to Mike's office."

"That was my third mistake," I correct her, counting with my fingers. "My first one was talking to Isaiah in the first place. The second was keeping Theo waiting. Going to see Mike was most definitely third."

She looks over my various bruises. "Mighty big third, though."

"Agreed."

Her eyes flicker over to the clock on my nightstand. "I have to go. I'll come back and check on you tonight, okay?"

I nod. "I imagine I'll still be here."

I spend the rest of the day in my apartment. I soak in my tub. Redo my nails. And even read a bit. I think about Isaiah and what I'm going to do about him. Try to decide if I should attempt to see him again. Vicki brings pizza when she comes back to my apartment hours later. We don't often have enough time to sit and talk, and she has plenty to say about Isaiah and me.

She lets out a low whistle and shakes her head when I bring him up. "Girl, I don't know what alien's taken over your mind, but you better find a way to get them out."

"My body hasn't been invaded by aliens," I said. "I just thought I could see him one more time..."

Vicki continues shaking her head. "Oh, no."

"What?"

"Let me summarize," she says. "Your old boyfriend comes to town. He's a pastor. You're a hooker. That enough for you?"

"He doesn't *know* I'm a hooker."

"Right," she says. "Have you given any thought to what this patron saint of All Things Perfect is going to do when he finds out his old childhood friend is a whore?" She's been talking rather calmly, but as she's continued, her voice has gotten higher and higher. By the time she gets to the end of her sentence, she's basically yelling.

I squint. "I'd rather hoped to avoid that issue altogether."

"And just how did you envision doing that?" She sits with her arms crossed.

I feel like I'm a teenager, getting the third degree from a parent before heading out for a night out. "I don't know," I say.

"Listen to me, Athena," she says, leaning forward. "I love you like the sister I never had, and I'm closer to you than probably any person on earth. I don't say that just because I've seen you naked more times than I care to remember. But this has got to stop. I don't know what's been going on with you the last few days, but snap out of it."

I stand up. "Thank you so much for your opinion, Sugar, but I think it's time you left."

She doesn't budge. "Don't pull that Sugar crap with me."

"I don't know what you're talking about."

She stands up and glares at me. "You know exactly what I'm talking about. This Southern Belle/Sugar thing you do when you try to hide what you're really feeling. You forget I've known you way too long. I see right through you."

She's right, of course. I know she is, but it just hurts. It hurts that Isaiah's not going to want anything to do with me once he knows the truth. I just have to make sure he never finds out.

"I'm tired," I say. "I think I'm going to go to bed."

"When it all turns south — and it will —" She walks to the door. "I guess I'll be here to help you pick up the pieces. But keep in mind, I won't be here forever."

I crawl into bed, but I'm not able to sleep. I keep trying to remember if it was really Isaiah I heard while I was out. Was it real or my imagination? Parts of that time seem so vivid to me, almost as if I can reach out and touch them. But others are fuzzy, and I can't separate fiction from reality. I finally give up and fall into a restless sleep.

A loud, steady pounding on my door wakes me the next morning. I groan and look at my alarm clock. Eight-thirty. Much too early to be awake considering it had been after four by the time I was finally able to fall asleep last night.

This morning. Whatever.

The pounding continues.

"Just a minute," I yell. I jerk my robe on, punching my arms through the holes, and belt it around my waist. Another pounding knock. "I said I'm coming!"

I don't bother to look out my peep hole. It has to be Vicki and I'm going to kill her. I fling the door open. "What?"

Mike stands there, hand raised to knock again, and looking like the devil himself. "About time."

I belt the robe around my waist tighter. Why the fuck is he here?

"Sorry," I say. "I didn't know it was you."

He raises an eyebrow.

"Sorry, *Sir*," I correct myself.

He nods, and I move aside so he can enter my apartment. I can't imagine what would bring him here. I can count on one hand the times he's stopped by in the last few years.

"Can I get you something?" I ask.

He ignores me, walking instead around my couch, looking closely at my bookshelves and running a finger along the books. His finger drops to my collection of movies. "Don't happen to have *Pretty Woman* here, do you?"

"No, Sir," I say, still irritated and tired and not thinking straight at all. "Never much cared for fantasy."

He gives a low laugh that sends warning signs through my body. "Still a bit cheeky, are we?"

"Just honest." I hope I'm not pushing his buttons. It's just so early and I'm sore, and if I could just sleep a little bit longer. . .

My head jerks up to look into his eyes. Mike wouldn't come by just to chit-chat. He has a purpose for being here. I vaguely remember the person I thought was Isaiah bringing me home. What if Mike meant to kill me that day and now he's here to finish the job?

Fear seeps into my spine and trickles down. I can't find the words to ask him. After our last meeting, I'm not sure I'll ever ask him anything again.

Mike, of course, knows this. "Ask me," he says, his eyes dark and dangerous.

I straighten my shoulders, blow a strand of hair out of my face, and refuse to give him the satisfaction of knowing just how much he scares me.

"What can I do for you, Sir?" I ask, my deadpan tone matching his.

He doesn't answer me. Instead, he continues his walk past my bookcases and moves around to the front of my couch. "Sit down."

Because he's a power freak and will never sit down while I'm standing. I don't even think about disobeying. I walk over and sit down.

It's not until he very slowly and very deliberately draws every bit of tension possible from the moment that he sits down himself.

That has to be a good sign, I tell myself. He can't kill me if he's sitting down, can he? Unless he has a gun. I squint. Does he have a gun?

I cross my legs and kick my foot up and down, bouncing an imaginary strappy sandal. He won't get the best of me this time. I'll sit here for as long as it takes him to get to his point. Longer, if I need to. I start counting in my head: one Mississippi, two Mississippi, three Mississippi. . .I'm up to ten Mississippi before he breaks the silence.

"I had an interesting conversation with Isaiah Martin last night."

My foot stops bouncing.

Isaiah.

I shouldn't care. Thinking about Isaiah, much less talking with Mike about Isaiah, has brought me nothing but trouble. One of these days I'll learn.

Just, you know, not quite yet.

"Oh?" I ask, hoping I'm instilling enough I-Could-Care-Less attitude in that one syllable.

But as much as I try for *I don't care* in my tone, my mind works franticly. *Why had he met with Isaiah? What did they talk about? Why had he felt the need to come to my room to tell me about it?* I look back at his eyes. Still dark and dangerous.

Don't ask. Don't ask. Don't ask.

"How's Isaiah doing?" The question flies out of my mouth, not caring at all how my head feels.

Victory surges in his eyes and I curse my mouth for not listening and myself for not having more self control.

His response, when it comes, is very thought out, very deliberate. "I wasn't surprised you didn't tell your childhood friend exactly what you are."

It hits me then, why he's here. I'm not going to have to worry about telling Isaiah I'm a prostitute. Mike has already done so and came by to gloat.

But Mike isn't finished yet.

"Isaiah has the potential to be a man of influence in the community," he continued, "And it would be a good idea for me to be on his good side. I asked myself, what could I do? What could I offer to ingratiate such a man? What could he want?"

Why he came by my apartment is now clear. What he'd decided last night that he could offer Isaiah hurt more than what he'd done to me days before. I can only hope my guess is incorrect.

He shrugs. "I offered him you."

With those simple words, it's like he's doused me in ice water. My body is frozen and I want to cry. But I'll be damned if I do so in front of Mike.

Oh, no. Not Isaiah. Please, God. Please, anyone but Isaiah.

I think of Mike offering my body to Isaiah. Like I'm something to be bought or sold or given away.

And at that moment I realize the truth of what I am, of what I've become. I *am* a commodity to be bought or sold or given away. Mike can give me to Isaiah or use me, because that is the right I've given him. I vow to take it all back. No matter what it costs me, no longer how long it takes, I'm taking it all back.

Before I unintentionally expose my new revelation to Mike, I drop my eyes in pretend submission. Close them and force my body to stop its inner trembling.

"Ask me what he said." His tone of voice leaves me no choice but to obey.

"What did he say?" I ask, all the while looking at my carpet. Out of here, I promise myself, I'll find a way out of here.

"Look at me." Amusement fills his eyes when I look up. His mouth twists into a horrific smile. One I remember all too well. "He said no." Before relief can sweep over me, he adds, "He asked to use the piano in Playmakers instead."

An evil laugh fills the confines of my room, and the walls feel smaller than ever before. "You must be the worst kind of whore there is," he says. "To be desired less than a piano."

I can't go back to sleep after Mike leaves. My cozy apartment is feeling like a prison, and I have to get out and escape for a few hours. I dress carefully, doing my best to cover my bruises and step outside inhaling deeply. Though I normally stay away from it, I decide to head for the Strip. For some reason I find myself longing for the crowds. I want to lose myself in a mass of strangers. I have to get away from the solitude for a few hours.

I walk for half an hour. It's one of those standard hot as hell, dry to the bone days and I'm not used to being outside much. But the thought of going back to my apartment isn't appealing, I want to stay in the open air. Where I can at least pretend for a few minutes that my life isn't what it is. There's a bench near the Bellagio that's my thinking spot. I head toward it.

It isn't surprising that someone is on my bench. After all, it is Vegas and the Bellagio is a nice place to sit and rest for a bit. What is surprising is the person sitting on it.

Isaiah Martin.

Chapter Five

My first thought is that it's a setup and Mike's somewhere nearby watching. It's without a doubt something he'd do: make a rule and then tempt me to break it. I glance around to make sure he's not nearby. I even try to peek into the windows of the buildings that look out onto the bench, but of course, I can't see anything.

I still don't move. It's like my feet are encased in cement. Only when someone bumps into me do I realize I'm standing in the middle of the sidewalk.

"Watch it," the person who bumped into me says.

"Sorry," I reply. I plan to walk past my bench and pretend as if I don't see Isaiah.

But of course, right when I'm within a few feet of where he's sitting, he looks up.

"Athena."

Damn. Damn. Damn.

"Isaiah," I say, hoping I'm wrong and Mike isn't nearby. And then it hits me: Why would Mike be nearby? It's not like he's following Isaiah around just to see if I'm going to show up. My smile for Isaiah grows bigger.

"Come have a seat." He scoots over to make room for me.

I tentatively sit down and his eyes widen as I remember my visible bruises.

He reaches a hand up, but hesitates and doesn't touch me at my slight flinch. "What happened?"

I touch a spot that's still sensitive on my cheek, probably the one he's looking at. I finger it gently. "Oh, that. It's nothing."

"From the party?"

"Huh?"

"The party you were on your way to when I ran into you at the hotel the other night."

Right. I'd told him I'd been going to a party. "Yes," I say. "It was a bit wild. Dancing, you know? One of my girlfriends swung her arms a bit too vigorously."

"And hit your cheek?"

"We were dancing really close." I can't decide if I want to let on that I know Mike told him what I do.

"I know you weren't at a party," he says. "Mike told me."

His voice doesn't hold any judgement, but I still feel shame. "I didn't want you to know. Not yet anyway."

"Did it happen when you were sixteen?"

"Yes, it's a long story. I don't want to go into it."

He nods, but I get the impression he knows there's more I'm not telling him. I need to change the subject. Get the focus off of me and my job and how I look.

"How's the church going?" I ask.

"Set up's slow, but the first service is Sunday. If you'd like to attend, you're more than welcome. Playmaker's Lounge at ten o'clock." He smiles the sweet smile that reminds me of my childhood, and the sight of it hurts something in my chest. "It'll be nice to know at least one person."

I swallow my snort before I offend him. He's trying to be nice, and while I appreciate that, there's no way in fucking hell I'm going to church. Casino or not. "I'll have to wait and see."

"It's so hot here," he says changing the subject. "You've been here ten years. I can't imagine being here that long. It's so different from home."

I shrug. "I've gotten used to it over the years."

"I guess I'll get there eventually."

"You will," I assure him and I want to kick myself. What am I doing? Why am I trying to help? I should be doing everything in my power to get him to go back home.

"It's so good to talk to someone from home." He leans forward, inching closer. "You have no idea how hard it's been. Moving here. I haven't met very many people yet."

If I wasn't a prostitute, this would be my cue to ask him for a lunch date. We'd meet at a nearby deli and talk and get to know each other all over again. But I am a prostitute. One who has explicit orders not to be around Isaiah Martin. And while it's possible luck will be on my side and I'll be able to have this moment without Mike finding out, there's not a chance in hell I'm going to tempt fate by meeting him again.

"I'm sure you'll soon have more friends than you know what do with," I say.

"Can we meet tomorrow?"

I shake my head and start to stand. "No, I'm sorry."

He narrows his eyes, analyzing my reply. Does he see through me? "No problem. Later then."

Yes, later. Like never later.

But I nod. "I look forward to it."

I'm walking back to my apartment, replaying the conversation with Isaiah in my mind. I don't plan on seeing him again, and I want to catalogue every moment, every detail, so I can recall it years from now. Hold on to the part of me that was once normal and free.

Something's off, though, and I dig further into the conversation to try to find it. Isaiah had been a perfect gentleman. Such a change from what I'm used to. I replay his words, and it hits me.

I never told him I'd been in Vegas for ten years.

I'm conflicted by the emotions running through my head. How could he possibly know how long I've been in Vegas? I finally convince myself that he'd simply done the math, or Mike told him. That was probably how he knew. I bet Mike really enjoyed telling him exactly how long I'd been a hooker. There's no other explanation.

I'm so focused on Isaiah, I don't see him until it's too late.

"Athena."

Harris is standing in front of my apartment, and I hate myself, because for a second I was thinking about how nice looking he is. He has an easygoing self confidence about him that doesn't seem diminished when he's around Mike, and that's more than you can say about most people. Plus, there's the way his eyes always seem to dance, almost like he knows what's going to happen before it does.

Idiot.

How can I possibly think such a thing about Mike's second in command? His eyes? Seriously.

I toss my hair behind my shoulder. "What do you want?"

"What I want has nothing to do with this visit."

"Right," I say. "You're nothing but a message boy. What does your big, bad boss want?"

I think I see a slight flash of amusement in his expression before he scowls. "You need to watch the way you talk to him, Athena. Unless you want a repeat —"

I wave my hand to shut him up. "Save it. What does he want?"

"He wants to see you in his hotel office."

My stomach falls to my feet, and the earth tilts.

I hear Harris mumble, "Damn it," and seconds before I fall down, he grabs me and brings me to my feet.

"I'm fine." I try to push him away, but he doesn't listen and for a few precious seconds I lean on him. He's strong. I feel hard muscle under his shirt. The way he's holding me isn't sexual, and it's a very odd, almost comforting feeling.

"You're not fine," he whispers, those knowing eyes of his searching my face. *For what?* "Come with me, Athena. Let me take you from here. Let's leave."

If it weren't for his two arms around me, I would probably slide to the ground. *What the fuck?* "Are you insane?" I ask. "He'd kill us both."

"I can protect you."

I hesitate for a second, pretending his offer was real and possibly just that easy. But I'm not new to the way this game's played. "I know what you're doing. You're trying to trick me. I'm not stupid."

I push him away and start walking toward the hotel, but my legs are weak and wobbly. Within a few seconds, Harris falls in step beside me.

"I'm sorry, that was out of line," he says.

"Damn straight." I wish he wasn't walking with me. I need time to get back inside my head, to prepare for the meeting I have facing me. I don't allow myself to think about why Mike wants me. There's nothing good that will come from trying to figure it out.

However, instead of building up the wall I need to face Mike, the wrong thoughts run through my head: Isaiah and how much I really want to have lunch with him tomorrow, Harris and how in the deepest, darkest place in my soul, I want his offer to run away to be for real.

Fortunately, he doesn't talk anymore on the way to the hotel, and I manage to pull together somewhat of a breezy, I-don't-care attitude once I make it to Mike's office. I turn and look over my shoulder.

Harris is texting. I can probably guess what it says.

She didn't fall for the 'Let's run away' ruse.

I glare at him. Bastard.

Chapter Six

I find I'm unable to keep up my nonchalant attitude once I knock on Mike's office door in the hotel. I'm visibly shaking. I wish more than anything I could stop so Mike won't know how terrified I am to see him again.

"Come in," he calls in reply to my knock.

I open the door and find him standing in front of his desk, arms crossed. I drop my eyes to the floor.

"Athena. Have a seat."

I risk a peek through my eyelashes. He doesn't look particularly angry. Maybe this won't go as badly as I fear. My breathing comes easier.

"Have a nice walk?" he asks and I gasp.

He nods toward a chair. "Sit."

I sit in a modern-looking chair that reminds me far too much of last time in his other office, and close my eyes. The shaking is even more pronounced. My entire body is one violent tremor.

"I believe I asked you a question."

I wonder if it hurts to die. "Yes, Sir, I had a nice walk."

His footsteps echo, but I keep my eyes closed, my head down, and count his steps. He moves ten steps away from me. Toward the window, if I remember the layout of this office. The room grows silent. After a few minutes, all I hear is the beating of my heart, the whoosh of air from my lungs, and the steady hum of his office refrigerator.

"I had an interesting conversation this morning. Led to an even more interesting request."

I can tell by the sound of his voice that he isn't facing me. I lift my head and open one eye. He's looking out the large span of picture windows, his back to me, arms still crossed.

This time, I tell myself I won't speak unless he asks me a direct question. I can't let him goad me into blurting out the first thing popping its way into my head.

I don't care. I don't care. I don't care.

I repeat my mantra a dozen times, but the truth is, I do care. If the conversation and request didn't concern me, I wouldn't be in this office. I bite the inside of my cheek to keep from asking.

He turns to face me, and even though I know better, I keep my eyes on him.

His smile is ugly.

"That must have been some performance you put on for Theo." He walks back toward me, and I force myself to keep my gaze steady. Focus on my breathing. "Much better than I would have expected after you were so horrifically late."

His words brought it all back: the meeting with Isaiah, the shock of seeing Harris, Theo's hungry gaze. I swallow hard.

Mike has reached me now, and he strokes my hair. "Hearing him talk reminded me of our early days."

I close my eyes against the onslaught of memories, but it does me no good. His fingers brush my cheek. "Remember?"

I don't want to. I don't want to remember the me who once was. How I'd looked at Mike like he was the answer to all my problems. How he seduced me into thinking he could do anything for me.

"Our first night." He is insistent today, and his fingers slide under my shirt. "You were so shy. You were perfect."

And he'd been gentle. I'd thought I was the luckiest girl on earth. Little by little, as he drew me in, he'd lost that gentleness.

"That night in the moonlight," he continues. His breath tickles my neck and my skin crawls, but I hold still. "Remember?"

I find myself sinking further and further into the depths of who I am. Slowly, my mind answers Mike's request and his relentless fingers. I am sixteen again, completely consumed by what I think will be the easy life. I am naïve and willing to do anything to charm the man I think will help me obtain that life.

"The first night I gave you to another. Remember?" he asks, and Isaiah slips away completely. The hands under my shirt grow rough.

"Yes," I whisper against the pain of the memory.

The hands stop. "Good girl."

He allows me a minute or two to compose myself, and it's not until he steps away that I feel the tears on my cheeks.

"I think today's walk will be the last of its kind for a bit," he finally says, and I nod helplessly.

"Besides," he continues. "I haven't had a chance to tell you about this morning."

I don't dare ask about the request. Instead I watch him walk to his desk and sit down.

"Theo was quite taken with your performance." He leans back slowly in his chair. His smile is still ugly. "He's going to be in town for a few days working with the new operation."

It would probably be a good idea if I knew what operation he was talking about, but at the moment, I'm too sore, tired, and emotionally drained. I just want him to spit it out and get on with telling me so I can go back to my apartment and take a nap.

"Once more I've decided you're out of the general rotation." He examines his well manicured fingernails. "Though not for the same reason as last time." He casually looks my way, and I can tell he notes my shiver at his sly reminder of what happened the last time he had me in his office. "Theo has asked for you to attend to him for the next week and I've accepted. You'll serve him exclusively starting tonight."

I work to keep my face unreadable. It's not an unheard of offer. Several times in the past I've participated in such an arrangement. Like all things in life, there are good parts and bad parts to consider. Though of course, the choice isn't mine to make.

"Well?" Mike asks. "What do you think?"

Normally, I'd reply with snark. Today, it would take too much effort. I only nod.

"And of course," he continues, "you'll get reimbursed. I think five hundred."

I bite the inside of my cheek. Five hundred dollars is nothing. It's a carrot dangled in front of me. I know from times past if I try to collect the money, he'll tell me he took 'expenses' out of it and pass me a twenty.

"Thank you," I force myself to reply and I know there's a bitterness to my voice.

"Never let it be said I don't take care of my girls."

There isn't anything to say to that, so I keep my mouth shut.

He reaches into his desk drawer and pulls out a room card. "This will get you into the Player's Suite."

I raise my eyebrow. The Player's Suite is the best room in the hotel.

He grins the same ugly grin. "I said I took care of my girls, didn't I? I knew you'd like the accommodations."

Actually, I like my own apartment, my own bed, my own sheets, my bookshelf, and my tub. His expression taunts me, practically begging me to say the smart ass comment dancing on my lips. I don't give in. "How very gracious. Thank you."

"There's nothing gracious about it, Theo is paying dearly." His eyes grow dangerous. "And you will too if this next week doesn't run as smoothly as possible."

I nod. "Yes, Sir."

He leans back in his chair. "Like I said before, there will be no more walks unless Theo asks you to accompany him. There will be no hanging out with Vicki. And most importantly, there will be no accidental meetings with Isaiah Martin." He pops his knuckles. "Understood?"

"Completely, Sir," I say, not really surprised that Mike knows everything.

"For the next week, you belong to Theo and you are to do any and all things he requires. If he tells you to do something, you are to act as though I'm telling you myself."

This isn't anything unheard of. Mike has all his clients sign a contract stating they understand what is and is not allowed. Still, even after all these years, hearing him say it aloud makes me shudder.

"Yes, Sir," I say again, but even I can tell my voice is lower.

"Good girl," he says, and I swear if I ever leave Vegas no one will ever say 'good girl' to me again.

"Now." He's either completely unaware of my dislike of him or choosing to ignore it. "You look a bit rough. I need you to go rest and pack so you can show Theo a good time." He nods to the passkey in my hand. "Be in his room by seven. Not seven fifteen or even five after. Seven exactly."

When he turns back to his laptop and doesn't say anything further, I stand and walk to the door.

"Athena?" he calls in the second before I leave his office. "Isaiah Martin doesn't exist for you anymore."

I nod.

"I need a verbal response so I can be sure you understand. Say it."

I clench my teeth before replying, "Yes, Sir. I understand. Isaiah Martin doesn't exist for me anymore."

I am certain he hears the hatred in my voice.

Chapter Seven

I trudge back to my apartment, feeling four times my age. In my mind, I'm thinking about what I have to pack for the week ahead, and I grit my teeth. I won't have any down time at all; at no time can Theo see me as anything less than the most desirable woman he's ever laid eyes on.

"There you are. Where have you been?"

My head shoots up at the desperation in Vicki's voice. Her eyes are bloodshot and her cheeks wet.

"Vicki? You okay?" I fumble with my key and let us both inside.

She doesn't answer until I close the door behind us. "Something's going on."

"What?" I ask, but her eyes dart around the apartment. "Vicki?"

"Do you think our places are bugged?"

"What? No," I say, but my mind can't rule out the possibility.

She bites her lip and turns on my kitchen faucet. "Come talk over here, they won't be able to hear us over the water."

"Are you insane?" But I walk over to stand by her anyway. "Now will you tell me what's going on?"

She shakes her head. "Where were you?"

"I went out this morning and when I came back, I was summoned to Mike's office."

She drops her head low toward the water running into the sink. "Again?"

"I wasn't called the first time. I went of my own accord." I'm trying to figure out what's going on with Vicki, but I don't have a clue as to what her deal is. The last time I saw her, she wasn't like this. It scares me.

But even more so, I'm scared about what will happen if I'm late tonight. I need to get my suitcase, pack, pull my shoes together, probably do my nails. And I really needed a nap. I glance back to Vicki, still standing with her head in my sink.

"I really need to get busy," I tell her.

She doesn't move her head. "This early in the day?"

"I have to be at hotel at seven. Exactly."

"How long?"

"A week. Now would you get your head out of my sink?"

She stands up and water drips from the ends of her hair. "You need to come over here."

I'm not sure why I keep discounting her warnings. I blame it on the emotions of the day catching up. And the fact that Mike somehow knows everything. I decide some of the blame is Theo's as well, because why not?

""Vicki, seriously, stop."

She leans further into the sink. "I'm telling you, something's going on."

I walk to my tiny closet and jerk out a suitcase. "You've been one of Mike's girls for eight, maybe nine years, and now all of a sudden, you're worried about someone bugging your apartment?"

"Honestly, I think — "

"Can we talk later? I'm exhausted and have too much to do to sit around with my head in a sink."

She slams the one-handed lever on my faucet so hard, I'm surprised it doesn't fall off. "Fine. Later."

I sigh. Great. Now, I've pissed her off. Strike two hundred three for me today.

"Look." I reach out a hand, but she bats it away. "I'm sure I'll have some down time at some point this week. I'll talk to you then. I bet the Player's Suite isn't bugged."

Her lips tighten into a thin line. “I bet it is.”

“Then maybe we'll have a chance to talk outside.” I walk to the door and open it.

She wipes an eye. “You don't believe me, do you?”

“I'm tired. I'm sore. I have to pack. Dealing with one more thing will send me so far over the edge, I may not find my way back.”

“Of course,” she says. “It's all about you anyway."

She leaves without looking at me again.

Chapter Eight

My time with Theo isn't that bad. Granted, it isn't all that good, but comparatively speaking, he's not the worst I've been with. Not by a long shot. During the day, he works from the tiny office in the suite, and in the evening we go out.

Whenever we're out in public, if he's able, he keeps his hand on my thigh, as if I'm going to bolt if given the opportunity. Nights are nights. At times, he is rough and demanding. More often than not, I wake up tired and sore.

Halfway into our week, Theo opens the door to the bathroom and finds me soaking in the tub. I've just taken some ibuprofen and am trying to soak the soreness out of my muscles.

"We're doing dinner downstairs tonight," he says, eyes skimming over my body. I don't even bother trying to cover up. "We leave in two hours."

Play your part.

I bring the washcloth up to my upper chest and squeeze, letting the water run over my body. "What would you like me to wear?"

His eyes are fixed on my chest. "I'd like for you to wear nothing, but that would probably get us kicked out of the restaurant. Do you have anything suitable for an upscale bistro?"

I come to my knees, choking back the ever-growing resentment and hatred. "Sugar, I've got anything you want."

He undoes his pants. "Come here and prove it."

I feel out-of-sorts and uncomfortable in my own skin at dinner with Theo. I look well enough in my classically simple black dress and spiked heels, but on the inside, I feel itchy.

I have to play my part, though, and I make myself focus on dinner and the man across the table from me. We're sitting at a table near the center of the restaurant's dinning area. A prime location to see and be seen. No doubt part of Theo's intent.

The waiter, a young man I recognize from previous dinners, waits on our table, and after he takes our entrée orders, I realize I've said less than ten words to Theo. Not a wise move considering my recent run-in with Mike. I clear my throat, and Theo looks up from swirling his wine glass.

"So, Sugar," I say. "Tell me again what it is you do."

He immediately launches into a near monolog about his business, allowing me the opportunity to 'ooh' and 'aah' at the appropriate times. Simple as that. He gets to talk about himself, and I pretend to listen and pay attention. I mean, really, what harm does it do? It's not like there's going to be a quiz at the end of the night.

While Theo drones on and on about all the great and wonderful things he's done for his company, I tune into the nearby conversations of the diners around us. It never hurts to be in the know about what's happening around you, after all.

A deep laugh catches my attention. I smile at Theo, run one finger around the rim of my water glass, and delicately look to my right.

Isaiah.

Two tables away.

I place my hands in my lap, afraid I'm going to knock my glass over.

I hope he doesn't see me.

Theo stops talking long enough to take a bite of his salad. Fortunately, he's so caught up in telling the story of himself, he doesn't notice my inattention.

I smile at him. "That sounds absolutely fascinating." Though, truthfully, I have no idea what he's been saying. For all I know, he spent the last few minutes reciting all fifty states and their capitals.

Fortunately for me, he must have spent a few words talking business, because he nods and starts again.

Blah. Blah. Blah.

I glance to my right again. Isaiah is dining with someone I don't recognize. I strain to see if I can hear what he's discussing, but it's no use. The dining room is too loud, and if I move my chair closer to the right, Theo will notice.

At the moment, he's bragging about something his vice president said.

"Unbelievable," I say, at what I hope is an appropriate time.

He snorts with self-satisfaction, and I risk another glimpse toward Isaiah's table. At the same time, I try to keep Theo's attention by pressing my shoe against his lower leg and running my foot up his shin.

And lock eyes with Isaiah.

For one long moment, neither one of us move. Then, his gaze travels to my outfit and flits across the table. Down to rest under the table where my foot still rests on Theo's calf.

Oh, no. Oh, no. Oh, no.

Nothing at first, but then understanding dawns, and Isaiah's mouth drops open. He closes it quickly. I spin my head back to Theo.

"Everything okay?" He glances around the dining room.

The room seems much too quiet.

"Just peachy, Sugar," I assure him. The me of two weeks earlier would have laughed and ran my hand across the table to subtly brush his fingers. Reassure him. Play him.

But I know Isaiah is watching my every move, so I drop my foot to the floor and give a toss of my head.

"I wonder where our food is?" I ask. *Pretend Isaiah isn't there.* "Feels like it's been ages since we ordered."

The undercurrent at the table has changed somehow, and even Theo is smart enough to notice.

He looks again in Isaiah's direction. "Maybe we should leave," he says.

"Oh, no." I reach my hand out and then pull it back before it can find purchase with his. "You don't want to miss the tuna. It's out of this world."

He gives one more quick glance around the dining room, scrutinizes my expression, and nods. "Why not," he says. "We have all the time in the world." He raises his glass. "To tonight."

Raise your glass, I tell myself. *Raise it.*

But my body knows Isaiah is still watching and in my mind, he'll know exactly what I'm toasting.

Across the table, Theo's eyes narrow. I fumble for my glass and in doing so, knock it over.

He lets out a string of cuss words and jumps up, dabbing his napkin at the ever-growing wet spot.

"Oh my word," I say. "Would you look at that? I am such a klutz. At least it's just water."

I take a deep breath and draw upon my ten years of experience. *Act like you're in control. Like you know what you're doing. That everything is going exactly like you planned.*

A waiter passes by and I hold out a hand to stop him. "Excuse me," I say, with a little wink. "I seemed to have knocked my water over. Be a dear and send a busboy over, would you?"

The waiter knows who I am, of course, but since everything in the hotel is one long, drawn-out play, he acts his part, gives a little bow and leaves with a gracious, "Yes, ma'am."

I turn my attention to Theo. "I am *so* sorry."

His expression hints at anger. His eyebrows wrinkle and his nostrils flare. "Well, then," he says, very serious like. Very dry. Very slowly. "We'll finish our dinner and you can make it up to me later."

I sit there and stare into Theo's You-Will-Make-Up-For-Spilling-Your-Water-And-I-Mean-Good expression, and I tell myself one way or another I am leaving Vegas.

Just play your part. Just play your part, I repeat the lines that have always gotten me through such times in the past. Gradually, I pull myself together. I give Theo my best seductive smile. "Sugar, by the time you close your eyes tonight, you won't even remember this."

The busboy shows up right at that second and artfully removes the soiled tablecloth. By the time new linens appear and my glass is refilled, the angry expression leaves Theo's face. We're finally alone, and I look to my right again. I first notice Isaiah, because he's who I'm looking for. But he's not looking at me, and I breathe a sigh of relief.

"Do you see someone you recognize?" Theo asks.

I snap my head back and mutter curse myself internally. What if Mike had tipped Theo off about Isaiah? That was all I needed. "No. Yes. What?" I stammer.

"At the table over there." Theo nods his head in Isaiah's direction. "Something or someone must have caught your attention."

I curse at myself some more, because not only is Theo pissed, I recognize who Isaiah is talking with.

Mike.

And Mike is watching me. I can handle this situation in various ways. For one, I can pretend I hadn't seen him, but our gazes had locked over Isaiah's head, so I'm sure that won't work. That leaves somehow acknowledging him. And after our time in his office, I know he won't appreciate bold and sassy.

Subtle and sly it is. And while it was never, ever, acceptable to lie, according to my Granny, all Southern women know the benefits of telling selective truths.

"It was nothing." I ignore Isaiah and give a quick wink to Mike. "Just someone I thought I knew."

Theo looks to my right and scans the crowd. I give his leg a gentle push under the table to turn his attention back to me.

"I'm still not sure if it's anyone I know." My foot moves further up his leg. I drag the heel of my shoe up his shin. "After all, what does it matter when I'm sitting here with you?"

Theo clears his throat, obviously caught off-guard. "Right," he says and turns back to his food.

I give myself a pat on the back. *Way to defuse the situation.* I pretend to take a sip of the wine the waiter inadvertently gave me after replacing the tablecloth.

Mike suddenly appears behind Theo and places a hand on his shoulder. "How's the dinner tonight?"

I thank my lucky stars I'd only pretended to sip my wine. Had I taken an actual drink, I'd probably spewed it all over myself. I wipe the smug grin off my face, replace it with a dutiful smile, and nod to Theo.

"Theo, Sugar." Fortunately, my voice doesn't shake. "How's dinner so far?"

Theo stands up and shakes Mike's hand."We had a little accident earlier, but it's all been taken care of. And Athena's assured me the tuna isn't to be missed."

"An accident?" Mike raises an eyebrow at me.

"Just a little spill," Theo replies.

"Do I need to," Mike looks straight at me, "*clean anything up*?"

"Oh, no," Theo answers, clearly missing the hidden subtext. "Your dining staff is superb."

"Yes," Mike says. "They are." The implication, of course, is his escort girls leave a lot to be desired. Theo, however, once again proves he's not the brightest light in the Vegas sky and completely ignores the subtle jab.

Mike chats with Theo for a few more minutes, and I force myself to look anywhere but in Isaiah's direction. The diners directly in front of me. The mural on the ceiling. My gaze follows our waiter to our table, and I watch as he places our entrees down. I'm not hungry anymore, and I know my tuna will taste like cardboard.

"I really hate to hear about your spill," Mike says to Theo. "Dinner's on the house tonight."

"Thank you." Theo pumps Mike's hand. "That's very nice of you."

Mike waves the compliment away. "Just like to see to my customers' satisfaction."

They finish their conversation. Theo sits down, cuts into his tuna, and starts eating. Mike slowly walks over to me. His hand is painful on my shoulder. He leans down and speaks low enough so Theo can't hear.

"Theo will be meeting with me tomorrow morning," he whispers. "He's very important to the new operation. His company is very important to the new operation. If he gives me any hint suggesting he is not one hundred and ten percent satisfied with the way this evening goes..." His grip tightens so hard on my shoulder I see stars. "I don't think I need to remind you of anything, do I?"

"No, Sir," I whisper.

"Excellent. Excellent." He pats my back and speaks louder. "You two have a pleasurable evening. You hear?"

Oh, yes. I hear loud and clear.

Chapter Nine

It's early morning by the time Theo finally rolls over and goes to sleep, but I'm not tired. There's not a part of me that isn't aching, yet it isn't pain that keeps me awake. It's the realization deep within my soul that if I don't leave, Mike will kill me one day.

When I was new in the business, I thought the danger would come from one of the men he set me up with. After all, you never fully know the danger that might reside in a person. Now, with years behind me, I believe I have the ability to read people.

Police officers worry about people shooting them. Firefighters might get caught in an uncontrollable fire. Hell, from what I've read, even CEOs have dangerous jobs; a good number of them die from coronary disease. How many prostitutes die on the job? I bet no one has ever run those stats.

Because who would miss a whore?

I stare up at the ceiling, and not only do I hate my life, I hate myself.

So now what? I ask myself. *Are you going to just keep on doing what Mike wants you to do, or are you going to make something happen? Take control of your life?*

It's fear that keeps people where they are. Even if things are bad, at least they're familiar. I keep staring at the ceiling, and it finally hits me that if Mike's going to kill me anyway, I might as well die trying to get away. Beats putting up with men like Theo every day and night of my life until Mike decides I'm not even good for that anymore.

It's a morbid thought, but it's what makes me creep out of bed and pull on a pair of jeans and T-shirt. I don't take anything else. If everything goes as planned, I won't need my things anyway, and if it ends badly... well, it won't matter.

I don't even take the room passkey with me. I tell myself there's no going back. I know exactly where I'm headed and what I'll find.

For the first time in ten years, I start to feel alive. Excitement pounds through my body, and I feel so light I swear I float down the elevator and toward the main entrance. No one even looks twice at me. Before I exit, I stop below one of the numerous video cameras and flip it the bird. "Fuck you, Mike," I mouth.

The temptation to run is strong, but I walk slowly to my destination. Behind the hotel, a small building lent itself to storage. I have in my possession a key, thanks to one of the security guys.

The truth is, I'd stolen it from him. But seriously, even if you list out all my vast number of sins, I doubt that one would even make the top twenty.

While Mike never paid us anywhere near what he said he would, he did on occasion pass us cash. And cash adds up over ten years. I don't use a bank because one of the girls did that and her account was mysteriously emptied. Likewise, Mike would find it if I kept it in my apartment, after all, the place is technically his. As I let myself into the building, I try to calculate how much money I've saved. My best guess is ten thousand. Nothing to sneeze at, surely, but a sad, sad amount when you think long and hard about it. Was I truly only worth a thousand dollars a year?

The metal door closes behind me with a clang, and it takes a second for my eyes to adjust to the low light. There's a small flashlight that I hid on a previous visit behind some boxes and I smile as my fingers wrap around it. The faint light trembles as I aim the flashlight to the row of crates along the back wall. Ten thousand dollars isn't a fortune, but it's enough for a plane ticket out of Vegas and rent money for a short while.

I tentatively push aside the crate in the far right corner, and the entire time my mind spins with all the places I can go. Not the South. Maybe someplace completely different, like Indiana. I can start over in Indiana, maybe work on my GED, get a job at a clothing store, a grocery store, a bookstore! My heart pounds as I imagine my new life.

With the crate out of my way, I wiggle the loose wooden wall panel. Will I settle in a big city, like Indianapolis, or go somewhere smaller? I can't decide. Maybe I'll rent a car once I land and check out a few places.

Hi, my name is Athena and I'm from Indiana.

I like the way it sounds in my head, and I giggle at the possibilities.

There's a hole a rodent made years ago behind the loose panel, I reach into it, feeling around, but my fingers only brush empty air. I frown and shift my weight. Wiggle my fingers deeper.

Nothing.

Oh, no.

The flashlight falls from my hands and I struggle to fit both hands into my hiding spot. It has to be there. It just has to be. Ten thousand dollars doesn't just disappear.

"Be there. Be there. Be there."

I rip the panel off and try to pry up the floorboard. Maybe it somehow got buried. Mentally, I calculate how long it's been since I've added money to my nest egg. Three weeks ago. No longer than four.

My fingers finally settle on a piece of paper. Heart beating wildly, I jerk it out, grab the flashlight, and read.

Do you think I'm stupid, Athena?

"No." The paper slips from my hands. "No, no, no, no, no."

I drop to the ground, choking back tears I know are going to fall anyway. Who would take my money? Who even knew where it was? The security guy I lifted the key from, Mike, or Harris?

In the end, it doesn't matter. Gone is gone, no matter whose hands it went through to get that way. My fingers scratch uselessly at the dusty floor, and hot tears stream down my face. Indiana will never happen. There will be no bookstore, no rental car. There is here and me and the men. I'll never leave.

"I don't want to be here," I half whisper, half choke. "I didn't know. I didn't know it'd be forever."

I'm not sure how long I sit there. By the time I finally emerge from the dark storeroom, there is a hint of the coming dawn teasing the horizon. There are people around, but no one seems to notice me, though I know I'm a sight with the puffy, red eyes.

I don't know where to go. I can't go back to the hotel. I can't even go back to my apartment. So I walk. And walk. With my head down, I can be anyone, going anywhere.

I wish I could walk forever. If I had my ten thousand dollars I would. But thoughts of my lost money bring the tears, and I sniffle, trying in vain to hold them back.

I look up to make sure I'm alone and unnoticed and find I've walked further than I thought. The hotel stands miles behind me, and tourist traffic has dwindled down to almost nothing. I take stock of my surroundings and head to a nearby public park.

I tell myself I'll just sit and think for a bit. Try to decide what to do while not thinking about how I lost ten thousand dollars overnight. But, of course, that isn't going to happen.

"It's Vegas, right?" I ask out loud. "Happens all the time. Probably a lot more than ten thousand."

I laugh, but it's not a happy sound that comes out of my mouth Matter-of-fact, it scares away the flock of pigeons who boldly approached to see if I had food.

"Sorry," I say, as they flitter away. "I didn't have anything anyway. Can't afford it."

How is it possible one person can make so many mistakes? I catalogue them: leaving for Vegas in the first place, trusting Mike, thinking my money was safer in the storage building and not my apartment. I sigh. No one's doing but my own. Make your bed and you have to sleep in it and all that jazz.

"Not that I do much sleeping," I mumble to myself.

"Talking to yourself?" a soft southern accented voice asks from behind me. "I've heard it's only dangerous if you answer."

I jump off the bench and spin around.

Isaiah stands behind the bench, hands in his pockets and his signature smile on his face.

"What are you doing here?" I ask.

Instead of answering, he comes around the bench, lifts an eyebrow and, at my nod, sits down. "I found this park a few weeks ago. It's not far from my condo. I like to come here early in the morning when it's just me."

"Sorry I interrupted your private time."

"There's no reason to apologize. What brings you out this early?"

He saw me at dinner with Theo, and Isaiah is smart man. He already knows what I am and what I do.

"I've had a bad day."

He gives a low whistle. "And it's only five in the morning. That's really bad."

He means it as a joke, but his words bring back just how alone and destitute I am. I'm not able to stop the sob that rips through my throat.

I drop my head into my hands and give into the tears once more. I curse myself for being such a crybaby, but that doesn't stop the tears. I cry, not caring that Isaiah is there, not caring if he gets up and leaves. Somehow, the cry is restorative. As the sobs lessen, I'm aware of a presence beside me. I sniffle and glance out of the corner of my eye. Isaiah. He hasn't left.

"Better?" he asks.

I shrug.

"Here." He hands me a cloth handkerchief. I take the soft piece of material and run my thumb along the monogrammed ISM. *Isaiah Samuel Martin.* I'm not sure what surprises me more: that Isaiah carries handkerchiefs or that he's letting me use it.

I hold it back out to him. "I'll mess it up."

"It's just cloth, Athena. Wipe your eyes, blow your nose if you want. You'll feel better."

I dab my eyes, just using a corner of the cloth.

"For goodness' sake." He snatches the handkerchief from me with one hand, holds my face with the other, and proceeds to wipe my face himself. All the time under his breath, he's mumbling. I hear something along the lines of 'stubborn woman' and 'piece of cloth'.

His hands are soft and gentle against my skin. When he brushes the handkerchief under my eyes, I close them, relishing his warmth. His touch is so different from what I'm used to. His fingers make me think of comfort and affection and something else that causes my stomach to flip flop.

"There," he whispers, and I open my eyes to find his face mere inches from mine. His hand still cups my chin, and his thumb traces my cheekbone.

"Thank you," I answer in my own whisper.

He swallows, glances at my lips, and drops his hands. "It was nothing." He scoots away as far as possible.

I glance down at my hands, unable to meet his expression. I hate that he's sorry he touched me. Even though we are alone in the park, it suddenly feels too stifling. I need to leave. To get away. Figure out what I'm going to do. I stand up.

He holds out hand. "Don't leave. I moved away because I didn't want you to think I was coming onto you."

"I'd never think that."

"Sit down and tell me why today's so bad."

I don't want to tell him too much about Mike. I don't know how close they are ,and I'm not stupid. I keep it simple. "I want out."

He nods. "Where are you going?"

"Nowhere, it seems. I've managed to save some money over the years. Not a lot, but enough to get me out of here. I went to get it," my voice drops, "it's gone."

"All of it?"

"All of it." I reach into my pocket. "There was a note."

He takes it from me and reads with a solemn expression. "Who would do this? How could anyone do this?"

"Real easy like."

His eyebrows wrinkle up. "It has to be someone who's watching you."

"I have a few ideas, but it's nothing I'm in a position to pursue."

He sighs. "You should call the police."

It sounds just like something a naïve know-it-all would say. "Did you miss the part about me not being in a position to pursue anything?"

"I guess I need you to explain it to me, because the way I see it, you're the victim of a crime and it's the police department's job to help you."

I glare at him, but can't find it in my heart to be angry. I guess for some people, life really is that black and white. Too bad the rest of us have to live with all the different hues in between.

"Look," I finally say when he continues to look at me with his hopeful expression. "I know you weren't born yesterday, and that in your world life is full of *this is right* and *this is wrong*, but you have understand that most of us live somewhere in between the two. The police won't listen to me. Even if they did, I have no way to prove that money was mine or even existed in the first place."

He drums his fingers on his thigh, and I see his mind spinning with ideas, possibilities he could offer. "I could talk to Mike –"

"No!" I jump up. I tremble just thinking about him talking to Mike. Of what Mike would do after.

"Mike and I are close, and he's powerful. He'll help, I'm sure." His expression looks decided. "I'll just explain –"

"What part of *no* don't you get?" So much for keeping Mike out of the conversation. "You don't know how Mike is. What he's capable of."

"He's a good man. He's helping me."

"He's evil."

"That's a bit much, don't you think?"

I stomp over so I'm in front of him and place my hands on my hips. "You don't believe me about Mike, and yet you think the police will believe someone stole ten grand from me?" I snort. "Yeah, I'm going to the police department. Right now. Know what? Forget I brought it up. I got myself into this, and I'll deal with it."

"I've upset you. I'm sorry."

My breathing is deep and heavy. "I just thought if anyone would believe me, it'd be you."

His eyes lock onto mine. "I believe you."

I sit down beside him again, making sure not to touch him in the process. "I'm still out ten grand."

Somehow, it feels better knowing he believes me. Granted, it doesn't feel good enough to make up for losing all my money, but I don't feel quite so alone. "I'm right back where I started."

"No. You're not."

"You're right. I'm worse off. Before, I had money."

"Don't you see?" he asks. "You've made an important decision. You decided to get out. To leave."

"Lot of good that's done, right? I can't leave if I don't have the means."

"I don't see why you can't just walk out."

"And go where?" I sigh. "It'll take me another ten years to save that much money again. I don't think I'll last that long. And I tried to leave once before."

He looks at me warily. "What happened?"

At the moment, I want nothing more than to soak in a hot, steamy bath. I feel so dirty. Truthfully, though, anything would better than sitting here talking about things I'd rather forget.

"I'd been in Vegas about a year and a half." I close my eyes, picturing the one other time I'd gathered up the nerve to leave. "I had a pocket full of cash and thought I'd head back home, try to finish school. But as I waited for the bus, I knew I didn't have enough money and that'd I'd be right back to selling myself."

"What did you do?"

I shrugged. "When the bus left, I was still here. Choking on exhaust fumes and trying not to look at Mike's self-satisfied expression when he walked outside to take me back."

"You never tried to leave again?" Isaiah asks.

"I thought about it a time or two, but never acted on it." I never told anyone so much about me, not even Vicki. Of course, I don't share with him how Mike forced me to show my 'gratitude' when he took me back.

"After a while, it gets easier to stick with what you know. The way I saw it, I had a nice room, food, clothes." A tear forces its way through my eyelids, even though I close them tight. "I just had. . . I just had to give pieces of myself away, night after night after night."

"Athena." He scoots closer to me, reaches out his hand.

"Don't touch me."

"I'll get you out," he says in a low voice. "I will."

"I'm not your problem."

"I never called you a problem."

I turn to face him fully. "But that's what I am, aren't I?" He'll never admit it, but he doesn't have to. I'm so tired of being seen a problem. I want to stand on my own, make my own choices, live my own life.

"You obviously need a place to stay. You can stay with me."

"Yeah, I'm sure the preacher bringing the hooker home will really make the neighbors pleased."

"Fortunately, I don't live my life trying to make my neighbors happy."

I don't even try to stop my sarcastic laugh. "And don't forget what your congregation will say because I'm not sure what Jesus would do, but I'm pretty sure it wouldn't involve Mary Magdalene, the Vegas Strip, and a condo."

"Now you're just being ridiculous."

He doesn't see it. I have to be ridiculous. It's the only thing keeping me from succumbing to another crying fit. Or maybe he does see it, because he doesn't wait for me to reply but takes me by the elbow.

"Come on," he says.

"Where are we going?" I try to yank my elbow away, but he's stronger than he looks. His fingers have a grip on me, and he's not letting go. You don't get that strong from sitting around meditating your way through life and writing sermons.

"Home," he says, and he loosens his grip a bit.

"I told you that's a horrible, rotten idea."

"And my other choice is what? To leave you here?"

Anyone else would. Anyone else would jump at the chance to leave me in the park. I don't like the hope that sparks inside my chest. I tell myself he's doing it because he's a preacher and he has to. That he wouldn't leave a dog alone in the park.

But it does no good. The hope is there, and like I'd recently discovered, hope is a dangerous thing.

Chapter Ten

He doesn't talk while we walk to his condo, which is fine with me. The silence allows me time to think. I wonder if Theo is awake and what he did when he saw I'd left. Does Mike know yet? Chills run up and down my arms at that thought, and I actually look over my shoulder, half expecting him to be there.

If I manage to stay out of his grasp, how long will I live looking over my shoulder? It's a sobering thought, and, truthfully, one I didn't think of when I decided to run.

But...

Am I'm really worth Mike's time and effort to track down? He has money coming in from everywhere; I'm just a speck of dirt in his sandbox. I probably bring in pennies compared to his other sources of income. No, I don't think financially I'm that much of a loss for Mike.

The cost to his pride is another issue altogether.

He may be willing to overlook my disappearance if he looks only at the money, but I'm willing to bet he won't. He's been in control of my life for ten years. He isn't about to give that up. He'll track me down to save face, and he won't stop until he finds me.

Isaiah walks with confident steps away from the park, his hand still cupping my elbow. I've brought him into this mess with Mike, and now he isn't safe either.

He turns down a street I don't recognize. How sad is it I know so very little about the city I've lived in for ten years? So many places I've never been: places I'm not welcome at or that I never have time to visit. There really is life beyond the Strip. Mike keeps us on such a short leash, probably because he knows if we saw everything, we'd never be content with him again.

Though I'm not sure *content* is the correct word.

It's not too much longer before we reach a set of nondescript condos. They're older and look a bit sad and rundown. The roofs need repair and paint is peeling in several places along the wooden trim. It's definitely a lower-middle-class neighborhood. Most of the cars parked in the spaces are older models, and many have dings and scratches. But for me, the entire scene represents freedom and a new start.

"It's not much, I know." He fumbles in his pocket for keys.

"It's perfect."

An old lady walking a tiny dog turns the corner, and her eyes latch onto me at once. I groan. I'm wearing jeans and a tee, but I'm sure she knows exactly how I earn my living. After a few years, we all seem to take on a certain look or have a certain vibe. At least, that's the way I feel. The dog barks and pulls at his leash as they get closer.

"Your neighbors are going to think you're paying me by the hour." I fidget in an effort not to pull at my shirt. *I'm just an average woman, standing here doing average things.*

"Sorry to burst your bubble, but you look like you've been to hell and back. Highly doubtful anyone is going to think you're leading me down the road to ruin." He waves to the lady. "Hello. Beautiful weather we're having, isn't it?"

"It's Nevada." She pulls the dog to a stop, which only makes him bark more. "It's hot." Her hawk-like gaze travels up and down my outfit. Her nose wrinkles, and she turns to Isaiah. I guess the average vibe didn't work. "I don't normally see you out when I walk."

"I'm usually out by six-thirty," he says with a smile, but it's not the smile I'm used to seeing. It's fake and doesn't light up his face.

The three of us stand there. She's not moving, and Isaiah isn't opening his door, though he has found the keys.

"Beatrice Brightman." She breaks the silence and holds out her free hand.

"Athena Hamilton." I shake her her hand. "I'm an old friend."

Her expression says she doubts that very much, but is far too polite to mention as much.

"Let's get you situated," Isaiah finally says and unlocks the door.

Beatrice's mouth drops open, and I take the opportunity to get a word in. "Nice meeting you." I glance down at the still-yapping dog. "And your dog."

She huffs, but pulls the little monster along, continuing on her way.

Isaiah watches her with an amused expression. "Lovely lady."

"You're a pastor. You're not supposed to lie."

He laughs and opens the door, stepping aside to let me pass by him. It's smaller than my place, filled with secondhand furniture, and someone on the floor above us is bouncing a basketball.

An old couch, probably slipcovered so often no one knows its original color, takes up most of the living room. I sit down; it's comfortable, though. He settles beside me and the couch shifts slightly under his weight.

My gaze falls on the one picture he has out. It's of his mom.

Isaiah's mother is descended from what we called Southern royalty. She can trace her family tree through several Confederate officers and her great-great-something fought the British in the Revolutionary War. I remember her as stark, stiff, and never without a strand of pearls.

My family wasn't rich, but my father worked as a manager in her in-law's company, and that made us acceptable enough in her eyes. My mom spent a lot of time trying to measure up to Mrs. Martin's exacting standards of Southern Womanhood. She always wanted the frosting on the cupcakes to be just right and the cucumber sandwiches to be cut just so.

"How is Mrs. Martin these days?" I ask.

There's a brief flash of surprise in his eyes, but it goes away when I nod to the picture.

"I haven't talked to her since I moved here. She's upset I decided to live in Sin City." He checks his phone and types something in. "Said if I had to be a preacher, couldn't I go somewhere worthwhile like the Congo?"

"She'd hate for you to go overseas."

"Of course. But it's more impressive to the Ladies Garden Club members if your son's a potential martyr in the wilds of Africa than if he's living the good life in Vegas."

"Your mom's sick."

"I like to say she's misguided."

I shrug. "Same difference."

He glances at his phone again. "I can't convince you to go to the police? You honestly think they're going to turn a blind eye?"

"No, I think they'd hold me, call Mike, and release me into his custody."

He shakes head. "If you'd just —"

I slam my hand onto the couch arm. "How many times do I have to say it? He buys the police. I'm such an idiot. I worried the entire way over that I was putting you in danger by being here, but I get it. Mike could show up with his entire entourage and you'd think he was coming for dinner."

"I'm sorry. I won't bring it up again. No more Mike."

"Thank you."

"If you don't mind a question, though, why did you stay so long?"

"I had nowhere to go. Still don't really. I can't live here forever. What am I going to do?"

He hesitates before reaching out and tucking a strand of hair behind my ear. "I don't know, but we'll think of something."

"There's one thing I'm good at. One thing I know how to do."

"No." His voice carries more force than I've heard before. "You're not going back to that."

"I'd say I'm not your problem, but I think we've had that conversation before."

"You're a fast learner."

"So I've been told."

His lips look soft, and I wonder how they'd taste. I've never wondered that in all the years and with all the men I've been with. Most of the time when I kiss a man, I taste alcohol. I bet Isaiah would taste like nothing I've ever had. Nothing I can even imagine.

He clears his throat.

I sit back. "Sorry."

He sighs and runs his hands through his hair.

"You need to get that mess cut," I say.

"I know. I need to find someone here to do it." He shakes his head. "Haven't had it cut since I moved here."

"I can do it." The words come out before I have time to think about them.

"Really?" His eyes widen in surprise.

I wave absentmindedly. "Sure, I did some of the girls' hair. Some of them said I did really good." I squint my eyes and force my gaze on his hair. "I think I could trim yours without doing much damage."

His lips uplift into a smile and I can't decide if he's trying to figure out how to let me down easy or trying to convince himself it's okay for a hooker — *ex-hooker,* I correct myself — to cut his hair.

I study his hair. It's so thick, I can only imagine how it would feel sliding between my fingers.

"Just a trim above your eyebrows." I tilt my head. "A bit off around your ears. The neck though." I reach without thinking and lightly brush where curls touch the nape of his neck. He jumps at the feel of my fingers. "Sorry." I scoot away.

"It's okay," he says. "It's just. . ."

"I know." I feel bad. I didn't meant to make him uncomfortable. "I forgot. I wasn't thinking." I want to keep the mood light so I add, "I think my own hair is in need of a cut."

You can't run from your past. I know that. Can't escape it, either. Have to face it. Very well, I can accept that. But that doesn't mean when I look at it, I have to recognize it.

"I see it as rearranging the future a bit." I pull my fingers through my hair. "Besides, this way I'll be less recognizable."

He doesn't appear sold on the idea, and I can't imagine why not. By changing my hair, I'll be taking a step in a new direction. A new me starts with a new look, right?

"Do you really think it'd be that easy?" he asks.

"What? Coloring my hair? Of course it's that easy. You can buy hair color anywhere. The hard part's deciding what color." I dig my fingers into my messy waves and fluff them. "I'm thinking red or brunette. How about you?"

His gaze is fixed on the wall behind me.

"Isaiah?"

He slowly looks at me. "I wasn't talking about the color."

"Okay, fine. What were you talking about?"

"Do you honestly think anyone who knows you would be fooled by a change in hair color? Especially someone with a more intimate knowledge of you?"

"I highly doubt I'm that memorable," I reply. "To most of them I was just a warm and willing body."

His phone rings then, and he glances down at the display and frowns. "I have to take this. Make yourself at home."

He walks into what I guess is the bedroom and closes the door, leaving me alone in the living room. I try to wait for him to get back, but my eyelids are so heavy, like all at once my body realizes how long it's been awake, and it's protesting staying that way. Was it only last night I had dinner with Theo? It seems as if it were days and days ago, not mere hours.

I yawn really wide. There's no sound from the room Isaiah went into. I don't know if he's still on the phone, but I don't want to bother him if he is. I'd like a blanket, but his condo is truly a bachelor pad, and there's not one to be found. I draw the line at looking through his closets.

My eyes struggle to stay open as I toe off my shoes and curl into a ball on the couch. I'm asleep within seconds.

Isaiah wakes me gently sometime later.

"Athena?" He rubs my shoulder. "I hate to wake you, but I'm afraid if I don't, you won't sleep tonight."

I groan, not ready to face whatever the rest of the day holds, but I sit up anyway. "What time is it?"

"Almost noon."

Wow, I slept longer than I thought I would. He's standing in front of me, and I smile at him. "I don't know if I said it already, but thank you. I know you didn't have to take me in."

"You're welcome. Now you've said it, so you're not allowed to thank me again."

I stretch. It feels so good to wake up and not dread the coming hours. My entire body feels light and the more I think about, the more it seeps into my brain that I've really left. I don't have the money to fly to Indiana and I may never work in a bookstore, but Mike doesn't own me anymore. He no longer gets to dictate what I do. The realization stuns me.

For the first time in ten years, my life is mine.

"That's an awfully big smile," Isaiah says.

"I'm free."

"You are."

I sigh and lift my arms above my head in an even bigger stretch. "I'm free." I like saying the word: *free, free, free.* My stomach growls.

He actually laughs this time.

"I'm also hungry," I admit.

"I can help with that, too. It just so happens I went to the grocery store yesterday. What are you in the mood for?"

I think back to the last meal I ate. I only picked at my food during that fateful meal with Theo. Lunch before that maybe? "I don't care," I tell Isaiah. "Anything sounds good at this point."

He crooks a finger at me and I follow him to the small kitchen. He opens the refrigerator and pulls out ham and cheese. Nodding to a cabinet he asks, "Can you get the bread? It's on the bottom shelf."

We pull out the necessary things to make sandwiches and it feels oddly domestic, but not in a weird way.

This is what my life would have been like if I'd made different choices.

Preparing a meal. Hanging out the kitchen. Making small talk about nothing at all.

You may not know what you're missing if you've never experienced it, and now that I'm having a taste of normal, I want it more than anything.

I don't talk much during lunch, my mind is still coming to terms with my new freedom. Trying to comprehend exactly what it means and I grow more and more excited with new realization.

People live like this. Everyday.

I wonder if they know how fortunate they are? Probably not, but I vow to never take it for granted. Not for an hour, a minute, or even a second. I promise to embrace every moment I have. To live.

"You're quiet," Isaiah says at one point.

"Just thinking." But the old me wonders if there's a hidden message in his statement. Does he want me to talk more? He's been kind enough to take me into his house. I should probably try to carry on a conversation.

"Do you have to go into work?" It strikes me that it's noon on a weekday. I can't claim to know a lot about what pastors do, but surely they have an office of some sort that they're expected to be at?

"I called them while you were sleeping to let them know I wouldn't be in today."

"You don't have to stay here on my account." Those are my words, but inside I'm secretly glad he is.

"I'll be fine as long as go in tomorrow. I don't want you to be alone today."

I don't thank him; he told me not to. "I don't feel like being alone."

As soon as the words leave my mouth, I realize how they sounded. "I mean, I didn't, I don't —"

"It's okay," he assures me. "I know what you meant."

"How uncomfortable is it to be a pastor with a hooker in your home?"

"It would only be uncomfortable if I cared what other people thought. Since I don't, I'm perfectly fine having an *ex*-hooker in my house."

I'm sure there are unwritten rules about a single preacher being alone anywhere with a woman of any age. But maybe not. Hell, what do I know? It's not like any religious types I'd been around had been paragons.

"I will have to go back to my office tomorrow," he continues. "Will you be okay here by yourself? Should I leave you the car?"

"I'll be fine. And, no, don't leave the car. If Mike were to come by looking, it might look suspicious if your car's here. Especially if it usually isn't."

He holds his head back, thinking about that for a few minutes. "That's very true. I wonder if he's been by today?"

My sandwich suddenly lodges in my throat at the thought of Mike being here, maybe looking into one of the windows.

"Damn it, Athena." He jumps up and puts his hand on my shoulder. "I didn't say that to scare you. Are you okay? You look so pale."

I swallow the sandwich and take a long drink of water. "I'm fine."

But my heart is still pounding and I keep looking toward the windows. Isaiah notices and frowns. He gets up to close them and pull the curtains. "I wish now I had a condo on the second floor."

Now that there's no light coming through the windows, the condo is dark.

"So what are we going to do?" I ask. "Sit around here in the dark all day?"

"I have some books if you'd like to read, or we can watch something on TV."

My ears perk up at the mention of books, and I happily lose myself for next few hours in Isaiah's small assortment. I don't regret for a minute the way I left my apartment and old life behind, but I do mourn the loss of my book collection. When I read, I can become anyone.

When you live day after day in despair, you need a diversion, or else you either go insane or kill yourself. I've seen both happen, and swore I'd never do either one. Alcohol only makes it worse. I drank heavily my first two years, but one day, one of Mike's girls went missing. All he said was that she was a drunk and no one wanted her anymore. He made sure he was looking at me when he said it. I stopped drinking that day, and books became my addiction of choice.

It's funny, in that sad sort of hopeless humor, it was because of books that I turned to drinking in the first place.

After I'd been with Mike for about six months, he finally decides it's time for me to be on my own. My new place is in a small complex not far from the hotel, and all of Mike's girls live nearby. I'm the newest, so I get the worst apartment.

My first night, I cry myself to sleep. The entire time, I think about how much I hate myself. Not because of my situation or because it's a shitty apartment. No, I hate myself because some sick part of me misses Mike.

He stays away for two weeks, and I hate myself even more when my heart pounds because he finally comes by to see me. He doesn't say anything, doesn't seem to notice how excited I am to see him. Calmly he steps inside, ignoring me to walk around the couch and glance over everything. His gaze travels to the bookshelf. Whoever was in the apartment before me left her books. I felt like I'd won the lottery when I discovered them.

"I told them to clear out all her things," he says with a nod toward the paperbacks.

"If it's okay, Sir, I'd like to keep them." I beg him silently in my head not to take away the books.

"I should probably have them burned. But, I don't know." He is amused and runs a finger along the spines. "A whore who reads Jane Austen might be a bit refreshing."

"Please."

His face has lost all signs of amusement when he turns back around. "How badly do you want to keep them, Athena?"

The lessons that stick with you are the ones hardest learned. That day I learned a lesson that would serve me well for the next nine years: don't feel anything and if you do, don't let it show. Emotions will be used against you.

I try to tell him it's okay, I don't want the books, but he saw my weakness and knows better. For months after that day, I can't think of a book without hearing in my head the slow slide of a man's zipper and feeling the choking hold of his hands around my throat as he pushes his way into me. I don't touch a book again for two years. Not until I stop drinking.

Isaiah and I spend the rest of the day in companionable silence. It's not until it's dark out that things become uncomfortable. He approaches me almost sheepishly.

"I'm going to let you have the bed tonight. I'll sleep out here." He's got an armful of bed linens and throws a pillow on the couch.

I look up from the book I've been reading. Of course. The sleeping arrangement. I should have anticipated this. "I can't kick you out of your bed. I'll take the couch."

"I'm not going to let you argue with me. I'm taking the couch. Besides, when I leave for work in the morning, if you're out here, I'll wake you up. This way you can sleep."

I can tell from his expression it's not worth arguing with him. One thing I've learned is that smart people chose their battles. This isn't a hill I want to die on, so I nod and say, "Thank you."

"I'm going to go ahead and try to get to sleep."

That's my cue to move to the bedroom. I take the book I'm reading and head that way.

"I put a new toothbrush out for you."

I don't even have a toothbrush to my name. But instead of dwelling on the negative, I focus on the positive: I have a safe place to sleep. I have food to eat. And I have a friend who will protect me.

I stay up late into the night reading. Old habits are hard to break, and I'm not accustomed to falling asleep until after two in the morning. My eyes finally feel heavy when I hear it. Someone's yelling.

I'm wide awake now, and my heart races because I can tell it's Isaiah. I have one thought:

Mike has found me. I reach for my phone, but realize I left it at the hotel with Theo, so instead I look around the sparsely decorated bedroom for something — *anything* —I can use as a weapon.

There's another yelp from the living room, and I run to the door and open it just enough for me to peek. It's dark, and I can't see anything, but there doesn't appear to be any sort of struggle going on. Perplexed, I crack the door more.

Isaiah's having a nightmare.

My hand clutches my chest in relief, but he groans in this sleep and starts to thrash around. I cross the room to him.

"Isaiah?" I touch his shoulder tentatively. "Wake up. You're having a nightmare."

"No!"

"Isaiah?"

His eyes snap open, and he grabs my wrist so hard it hurts. I jerk my hand back, but he doesn't let go.

"Ow, stop." I yank my arm again. "Isaiah. Let go."

He blinks. "Athena? What are you doing?"

"Waking you up. You were having a nightmare. Would you let go of my wrist?"

He seems to notice for the first time that he's holding me, because he lets go immediately. "Sorry."

"Damn, you have a grip." I rub my wrist with my other hand. I'm probably going to have bruises.

He sits up. "I'm so sorry. Let me see."

I take a place on the couch beside him and show him my wrist. "How'd a preacher boy like you get a grip like that?"

"I played football in school."

I laugh in spite of the pain in my wrist. There's no way the lanky Isaiah I remember played football. "You did not."

"I said I played. I didn't say I was any good. Anyway, I was at practice one day and I broke my arm."

Ah, yes. That makes sense. *That* I can easily picture. "I bet your mom flipped."

"Isaiah Samuel," he says in a perfect imitation of his mother's voice. "What did I tell you about contact sports? A gentleman with your ambition need not associate with ruffians."

I roll my eyes. "She didn't."

"She did. And just to piss her off more, I told her I'd changed majors and wasn't going to law school and didn't want to run for Congress."

"I wish I could have been a fly on the wall for that one."

"She got over it, eventually. I think. But that was the end of my football career. I kept working out though. I liked the way I felt. I lifted weights and ran. Still do."

"You run. On purpose?"

"Yes, ma'am. On purpose. Now let's look at that wrist."

He turns on a small lamp beside the couch and takes my hand in his. Carefully, he moves it from side to side. "Hurt?"

"Just a little."

"I'm sorry. I'm supposed to be helping you and keeping you safe. Not hurting you further."

"It's okay," I tell him, and it is. I mean, seriously. I've had much worse. But I can't get the words out because he's lifted my hand to his mouth and presses a kiss to the inside of my wrist.

I suck in a breath. It's a gentle kiss and completely unexpected. I'm ashamed that my first thought is that he must be expecting payment now. For letting me sleep in his house.

"Isaiah," I start. "I can't. It's —"

"Shhh. Let me do this. You can tell me to stop at any time and I will."

I close my eyes as his lips return to my wrist. He's only kissing my wrist. Nothing more. And I can stop him whenever I want. That, I tell myself, makes it different. I have a choice and I can stop this at any time.

I don't want to stop it. I want him to continue. I want to see if I can feel anything.

I've never enjoyed sex. Even my first time with Mike, before I found out who and what he was, wasn't pleasurable. Sex is something I do in much the way as I brush my teeth or wash my clothes. Except it's also an act, and I know exactly how to act like I'm enjoying it.

I don't want to act with Isaiah, but as his lips travel up my arm to the crook of my elbow, I suck in another breath. Not because it feels good or I'm turned on. It's because I feel nothing.

He shifts on the couch and presses me down on my back. "Are you okay with this?"

I nod. He gives me a small smile and slips his hand under my shirt. It's all I have on. After all, it's not like I packed to come here. I close my eyes and try to focus on what he's doing.

He takes his time exploring my body. His hands and lips are everywhere, and I can't help but compare him to what I've experienced in the past. There's a hesitancy with Isaiah the others didn't have. Like he's waiting for me to stop him.

I won't, of course. Sex is nothing to me. If he wants it, he can have it. At least he isn't going to hurt me. I run a hand down his back, and once more I'm shocked by how muscular he is.

"Feels good having your hands on me," he murmurs against my skin.

He pushes my shirt up, and I lift myself allowing him to take it off completely. Once it falls to the floor, his eyes travel over me. "You're so damn beautiful."

I've heard it all before. Men tell me I'm beautiful everyday. I suppose I am on the outside. No one ever sees the inside, the not-so-beautiful parts. I steel my body, preparing for what comes next.

"Hey." His thumb brushes my cheek. "Where did you go?"

"I'm right here." I smile in a way I hope is seductive but he's frowning.

"No, you're not." He sits up.

It's ridiculous, but my first thought is, *No, don' t pull away. Mike will kill me.* Then it hits me: I'm with Isaiah and I don't belong to Mike anymore.

"I'm sorry." This is new for me. Apologizing for not being into sex. "I'm just so tired. I haven't been to sleep yet."

"I'm the one who should apologize. After all you've been through and I jump all over you like...."

He doesn't finish his sentence, but sits up and runs his fingers through his hair. "I'm such an ass."

I don't know what to say, but I know it's my fault. Everything was going so well, and then I messed it up. "I didn't want you to stop."

"Tonight's not the right time, Athena. Not like this."

"Another night?" I raise an eyebrow.

"Maybe."

"I'll take that on one condition."

"What's that?"

"Come to the bedroom with me. I don't want to sleep alone tonight."

He finally smiles. "I can do that."

We walk together to the bedroom, and when he gathers me in his arms, I think this is better than sex ever could be. I fall asleep quickly and sleep better than I have in years.

I eye his hair again the next afternoon when he gets home from work. "You need to let me cut that mess."

I've been inside his condo all day, and I'm going slightly stir crazy. Since he's been home, he's been in the bedroom making phone calls ,and I'm trying my best to be patient and not be a pain. But seriously? Couldn't he make the phone calls from the office?

"This?" He's sitting at the table and he hangs his head slightly. He sticks his fingers in his hair and rubs his scalp with a fury. When he brings his head back up, his hair sticks out everywhere.

I laugh. "That is a sight. It's also a disgrace."

"Completely unacceptable." His chair squeaks as he pushes back from the table. "I'll get the scissors."

He walks back into the kitchen moments later. He's changed into an old T-shirt and has a towel draped over his shoulders. "You sure you can shape this up? I'm not a vain man, but I don't want to look like I've been to a butcher."

I motion to the chair, and he obediently sits down. "I never had any complaints in the past, Preacher Boy."

He places a comb on the table. "That's because you had pointy metal scissors in your hands and they were afraid you'd stab them."

"Shut up and be still."

"Only because you're holding the scissors."

I straighten the towel around his shoulders, resisting the temptation to rub his back. He fills out the tight shirt and his shoulders move steadily with each breath. Is it my imagination or does a faint shudder run through him?

I close my eyes before touching his hair. Will it be as thick and silky as I think? Can I really do this? While I've cut some hair and trimmed a wig or two, I've never cut a man's hair before. Surely, it can't be that different.

I tentatively touch the top of his head. Run my fingers through the hair there. It's so much thicker than I imagined. Your average woman would die for such thick hair. My own is long and wavy, not as thick as his, but not thin and brittle either.

"You have nice hair," I say, all nonchalantly, like I don't want to spend all afternoon with my fingers buried in it. "You know, for a guy."

He snorts. "It covers my head. I can't complain."

I smack the back of his head. "You have hair like this and that's all you have to say? It covers your head? You are such a man."

"I decide to obsess over something on my person, it's not going to be my hair."

"Uh." I pick up the comb and work it through the tangled mess. "Now you sound all eighteenth-century. *Your person.*"

"I thought you'd appreciate the phrase. I saw you eye my collection of Henry James and Sherlock Holmes."

I run the comb and my fingers through his hair one last time before picking up the scissors. "They surprised me."

"What? That I read?"

I snip the ends from a section of hair I held in my left hand. So soft. How did a man's hair get so soft? "No. Yes. Maybe." I slap his shoulder. "I'm trying to concentrate here."

"Stop hitting me."

"Hush."

I bite my lower lip as I continue to snip ends. Slips of hair fall to the towel as I work, covering the soft terrycloth in patches of wispy brown strands. My fingers, the scissors, and comb work almost of their own accord. I tug his hair gently to ensure everything is even.

Satisfied, I take a step back to see better, and my gaze falls to the table. His hands rest in front of him, fists clenched so tightly his knuckles are white.

"Isaiah? You okay?"

He relaxes slightly. Or at least he unclenches his fists. "Yeah. Sorry."

It's because I was touching him, I'm certain of it. "I'm almost done."

His only response is a nod.

I go back to cutting his hair, but it's not the same. I can't concentrate on how nice it feels to touch him, to be near him, to breathe him in as if he's my own.

He's not.

I finish with his hair as quickly as I can. Snipping here and there. Brushing his shoulders ever so slightly. But my touches are quick and businesslike.

He relaxes and a deep breath escapes his body.

"Ta da." I step back, giving him room to stand. "All done."

He shakes his head. "Feels so much better."

"Wait till you see it."

"Why? Will I hate it?"

"No, I'd just rather you get the full effect before you start issuing compliments."

He turns, and his wicked grin is back. "Or complaints."

"No complaints, ever, remember?"

He nods toward my right hand. "Pointy, metal things, remember?"

I wave the scissors at him. "Into the bathroom with you and tell me what you think."

He laughs on his way down the hall and disappears into the bathroom. I bite the corner of my lips and wait for some sort of acknowledgement, good or bad. What if he hates it? Moments later, he reappears.

"It looks great," he says. "Thank you."

"Not just saying that because I still have the sharp, pointy things in my hand?"

"No, I think you did a fine job. I look all respectable again."

"You never stopped looking respectable." I gather the discarded towel and sweep the hair from the table onto the floor. *Unlike me.*

Something in my demeanor must give away the inner workings of my brain, because seconds later he touches my shoulder.

"Athena. Let me be your friend again."

His gentle touch brings tears to my eyes.

"We were never meant to be friends," I whisper. "We were meant. . . we were meant to be more."

His grip tightens.

Don't. Don't say it.

"I can't offer you more."

I knew what he would say, but the cut is still there – sharp and sure – yet, maybe not as deadly as I'd thought. I close my eyes and concentrate. If I try hard enough, I can rebuild part of my fortress.

Not enough, of course, it might never be enough again. Seeing Isaiah, talking to Isaiah, has changed me. I can accept that. But still, a few stones, stacked haphazardly, here and there. Maybe it'll be enough to get me back to where I can function again. To a place I won't be so vulnerable.

I push back the urge to throw my arms around him and instead focus on the anger. Anger at myself for letting the conversation with him go as far as it had. Anger at the men who kept me in work for all those years. And then, even though it's unfair, I funnel all that anger at him.

"You think I'm asking for more?" I say his eyes widen with surprise. "You think I have the privilege of asking a man for anything?"

Whatever he is going to say is interrupted by the ringing of his cell phone. He looks at the display and sighs. "I have to take this."

I nod, and he goes into the bedroom and closes the door. It shouldn't bother me, but it does. My mind knows he's a pastor and must have confidential meetings and talks with the people in his church. Talks that would be inappropriate for me to listen in on. But for some reason, it's almost as if he's keeping a secret.

Without him in the living room, the apartment is eerily quiet. Even though he was gone all day, it's such a stark contrast to what it was like mere minutes ago. It makes me nervous. I walk into the kitchen to see what I can find to make for dinner, but as I pass by a window, the headlights from a car sweep across the glass and I jump out of the way.

Has Mike figured out that I'm with Isaiah? If he thinks I've skipped town, he won't connect the two. But if he believes I'm still in town, he might. For all I know, that was him in the car that went past me. Or maybe Harris. He'd probably have Harris do the drive-by.

I'm sitting at the kitchen table when Isaiah comes out of the bedroom, and I must look like I feel, because the first thing out of his mouth is, "Are you okay?"

I don't want to bring up the conversation we were having before his phone rang, so I change the subject. "Has Mike asked you about me?"

He sits down across from me. "He called me at work today and said you were late for a meeting and if I saw you to let him know."

"How comfortable are you lying? It's not exactly a talent needed by the clergy."

"I think 'lying' is a strong term. I keep things confidential. It's totally different."

"If you were Catholic, I could tell you everything in confessional."

He cocked an eyebrow. "I hope you know enough about me to know I would keep anything you told me in the strictest confidence."

"I do," I said, not wanting him to think I didn't trust him. "I mean, I'm staying here. I'm basically trusting you with my life."

"I know that. Trust me."

That's been my problem. I'm always trusting the wrong people.

Chapter Eleven

A few days later, Isaiah presses some cash in my hand and tells me to go shopping. I push from my mind that I'm an impostor who doesn't belong in a mall, buying clothes like a normal person. But Isaiah is insistent, and even I can't argue with the fact that I need clothes. I've been wearing the same outfit over and over, washing it while Isaiah is at work.

So far, I've seen no hint of Mike searching for me. I'm hoping he thinks I had money hiding somewhere else and that I left the city days ago. I drive to the mall in the car Isaiah left for me. When I protested over breakfast, he told me he was walking to work. I'm pleased I only look over my shoulder a few times on my way.

I stand in front of a rack of sundresses shaking. It's not because I see Mike or anyone else. It's because I have no fucking clue what kind of clothes I like. What I like hasn't ever factored into what I've bought. What Mike likes, yes. What my clients would like, certainly. Me? Who cares?

I hold up a green dress. It's nice enough, but is it me? Maybe black? Or navy?

"May I help you?" A saleslady has managed to come up right next to me without my knowledge, and I jump at her voice.

"Sorry, didn't mean to scare you. Are you okay?" It's only taken her one look at my trembling hands, fingers clutched around colorful dresses for her to pick up on the fact that I'm way outside of where I belong.

"I don't know what color," I say in what has to be the lamest answer possible.

"Let's see." She holds up a gray one. "The color brings out your eyes, don't you think?"

Gray? I think it makes me look like a rock. Fitting, almost. I feel like a rock sometimes. Weighed down. Passed over. Cold. Dead.

What did cold and dead have to do with bringing out the color of my eyes?

She tilts her head and scrutinizes me more closely. "Hmmm. Maybe not. With your hair, I think a silver or ivory would be better."

My throat closes up at the mention of silver.

"Do you have any idea what that color does to you?" Mike is standing behind me and we're both looking in the mirror. I'm wearing a silver sheer nightgown and I'm scared for the first time since I've been with him.

One of his fingers traces my arm from elbow to shoulder and seductively moves across my chest and teases a nipple until it forms a peak.

"You're trembling. There's no need." He catches my eyes in the reflection of the mirror. "You're such a good girl, I just have to share you. I want him to see how good you are. You'll do it for me, right? Because you love me?"

They're rhetorical questions. I've already told him I didn't want to do it. But he becomes angry and quickly lets me know I have no choice.

"I've done so much for you," he says, still watching me in the mirror. "This is the least you can do for me."

"Fuck your friend?" I snap back. "That's me doing something for you?"

He slaps my face. "Yes. Now get out there."

"No silver," I choke out. My closet back at the apartment is filled with silver, because Mike decided the color looked best on me after that night. Silver gowns, silver lingerie, silver scraps of fabric all tailor made for a man's fantasies. "No way."

The sales lady politely ignores the terror in my voice and expression. "Ivory, then?"

Angels wear white, surely that means the fallen among them would be appropriately attired in ivory. We aren't as good as they are; we shouldn't be in the same color. Ivory, though, represents a lesser white, right?

The red is definitely out, though that's probably more appropriate. Pink is too...pink.

"There's a lot of thought going on in your head to be thinking on color," the lady says.

"I don't know, maybe this was a bad idea." If I can't even decide what color I like, how in the world am I going to function not being a prostitute?

"Shopping is never a bad idea."

The group of young teenagers who appear beside us certainly agrees with her. Loud, boisterous laughter floats up from them as they discuss boys, clothes, boys, shoes, and boys.

Watching them, I wonder if I had it to do over again, would I do it the same way? How had I gone on for so long living as I had? Why had I not seen before how my life had slowly been draining out of my body, as if some knife had pierced my heart and I walked around slowly bleeding to death? Perhaps when the wound's small enough, you don't notice it until it's too late.

"Ma'am?" the clerk asks. "Do you want to try those on?"

I look down to see I'm still clutching the dresses in a death grip, and I give her a sheepish grin. Damn, she must think I'm an idiot. "I think I need some coffee."

"Okay, coffee's always a good idea. My name's Cathy if you want to find me when you return. Should I hold one of these for you?"

That's probably a good idea. Isaiah isn't going to like it if I show up with nothing.

"Yes, thank you. I think the green one." I pass that one to her.

"Green would go lovely with your coloring."

Green. Green is my new favorite color.

I make my way to a busy coffee shop on the edge of the food court where I order a latte. I don't notice her at first when I sit down. It's only because of my relentless fear of seeing Mike that she happens to catch my eye as I glance around the seating area.

Young, pretty, and fidgeting slightly in her micro mini, nothing much stands out about her. I doubt anyone who hasn't been in her situation knows what she's getting ready to do. She stops twisting her hands in her lap and looks up. I follow her gaze to where a lone man stands, watching.

"Athena?"

I knock my coffee over, because it's Harris. He's found me.

Chapter Twelve

I quickly calculate how close he is to me and guess whether or not I have enough time to run. It's worth a shot, and I can always yell. I push my chair back and prepare to jump up and sprint away.

He sighs and sits down. "I had no idea you'd be so stupid to be seen out in public this soon."

His words surprise me so much, I drop back down in my chair. "What?"

"Someone might recognize you."

"You mean other than you?" I study him, watching for any signal he's getting ready to touch me. I'm still poised to leap.

"Yes. I've known where you've been since you left Theo's bed."

"Of course you have." And I'm an idiot to still be sitting here.

He leans toward me. "Flipping Mike the bird and telling him to fuck off probably wasn't the smartest thing you've ever done."

"You saw that, too?"

"Of course."

"And you're going to tell him you saw me here?"

He smiles and settles back into his chair. His body language gives the impression he's completely relaxed and wouldn't harm a flea. I know differently. "No."

"Why not?"

"I have my reasons."

"Which are?"

"None of your business."

I'm not sure I believe he's not going to tell Mike. He's his second in command; it's his job. But some part of me must believe him because I'm still sitting at the table with him. I exhale deeply, but the girl I'd seen before Harris came over stands up and walks to a window.

"Damn it," I say.

"Do you see someone you recognize?" Harris is suddenly on alert, looking around.

"Yes," I whisper. "Me. Ten years ago."

"Here?"

"Standing near the window at three o'clock." I don't want to point. Don't want to bring attention to either the young girl or myself.

"The one in the blue dress?" He doesn't wait for an answer, but continues on, "She's young."

Bile rises in my throat. "More naïve that way. Try to start them much older and they know too much."

There's a look of disgust on his face.

I nod to the guy standing off by himself, the first one I noticed. "See the guy in the black jeans?"

He shrugs. "Normal enough looking guy."

The worst ones usually look that way. They only grow ugly as you get to know them better. I close my eyes against the onslaught of memories.

"That's her Mike. She's young," I say, remembering, "fifteen maybe, no older than seventeen. Alone. That's a certainty. He's older, good-looking, and knows everything. She thinks she's in love. He's the solution to all her problems and has all the answers, even to questions she hasn't asked yet." Behind my closed eyelids, the girl in the mall becomes me and the guy with her becomes Mike. "He says if she loves him, she'll do this and she's too scared to say no. She's scared she'll lose him. Scared he'll leave."

"She'll do what?"

My eyes open; Harris is all blurry. "He wants to share her. With a friend of his. And she'll do it. But he won't be the last friend he shares her with. Not by a long shot." I sigh. "In the end, she'll turn out just like me: ten years older, sitting in a food court coffee shop, wondering why she's unable to decide by herself what color she likes."

Harris is silent, so I continue, "That's only if she's lucky, though." Pictures of girls work their way into my subconscious, desperate to be remembered. "Otherwise, she'll end up in an unmarked grave, collateral damage of a wild night, and no one will care. After all," my voice cracks, "she's just a whore. The world's better off without her, right?"

Across the table, Harris reaches his hand out, like he's going to take hold of mine, but he sees the shock in my eyes and stops. I look at the girl again, she's sat back down on the bench.

I turn my attention back to Harris. "You've really known where I've been this entire time?"

He nods. "It behooves me to know where you are."

"And yet, you haven't told Mike?" I try to think about why he would want to know where I was if he wasn't going to tell Mike.

But when he shakes his head, I know exactly why he hasn't told Mike. "You bastard. You think

I'm going to thank you for not telling him? By sleeping with you. Let me guess, you have a car outside you want me to follow you to and then after, you can just drop me off on Mike's doorstep."

For the first time since he sat down, he appears angry. "Jesus, Athena. How the hell do you come up with this stuff?"

"Tell me I'm wrong." I want to believe he's wrong. He's never looked at me with *that look.* The one men look at me with when they realize what I am. That's probably one of the only reasons I'm still at the table with him.

"You're wrong."

"Fine then." I cross my arms. "Tell me why you sat at my table to begin with."

"Answer one question first." At my nod, he continues. "Did Isaiah know you were coming here to shop?"

It's the most absurd question in the absolute most absurd conversation I've ever been in. It's so absurd, I don't hesitate to answer. "No. He just knew I was shopping. He didn't know where."

"That's why."

"Because Isaiah doesn't know where I am?"

"Exactly. Because I'm guessing it'd make him just a little upset to know you were in the same mall as the younger Mrs. Martin, his wife. Three tables away from her to be exact."

Chapter Thirteen

He's saying something else, but I can't make out what over the buzzing in my ears. I'm going to faint. I feel clammy, and spots dance before my eyes. The edge of my vision starts to go fuzzy, and someone is pushing my head down.

"Damn it." It's Harris and he's whispering. "Breathe. You better not pass out. That's all we need is for you to call attention to us."

I inhale deeply through my nose and exhale through my mouth. Little by little, things settle down a bit ,or at least I don't feel like I'm going to fall to the floor. anymore. Oh my God. Isaiah's married. Fucking married. It can't be true. I keep my head down for several more minutes, and when I look up, I'm furious.

"How dare you make something like that up? Seriously? Who does that?"

His lips tighten into a fine line. His blue eyes I once thought looked so good widen in surprise. "I'm not making it up. But I can understand why you might think I would." He nods to my left. "She's right there. In the yellow sundress."

I don't want to, but I can't help it. I slyly turn and look at her, anxious to see the woman who shares Isaiah's name. Supposedly.

My first impression is wholesomeness. Everything about her screams the word with her- shiny brown hair and friendly brown eyes. She's having lunch with someone, and she's smiling at what the other woman is saying. Her skin has a faint tan, probably from sunbathing too frequently in the Vegas sun. I smile a little, the famous dry heat of the Southwest obviously took her by surprise. Not an uncommon occurrence for Southern belles. It's clear that's what she is. The food court isn't that crowded. I can hear the faint cadence of the accent she shares with Isaiah.

Everything about her brands her as the type of woman Isaiah wants. Which is everything I'm not. Hell, she was probably a virgin when they got married. I really want to hate her.

She lifts her cup to her mouth and my gaze falls on her left hand. A small diamond and thin gold band grace her ring finger. I mutter a curse under my breath.

"Her name's Lydia. She's a nurse. Works in the NICU at Valley," Harris says.

It's too good to be true. She has to be the most perfect woman on the planet - beautiful, happily married, a pastor's wife, *and* she cares for severely sick infants. She probably conducts cancer research in her garage during her off hours.

But again, nothing he's saying adds up. The dots don't connect.

I glare at Harris. "I know you're lying. I've been at Isaiah's condo for the last few days. He's not married. His place has obviously never had a woman in it. I can't imagine a more typical bachelor pad."

"Right, because he's really going to take you to the house where he keeps his wife. Fuck, Athena, were you born yesterday?" He's pleading with me. For some reason he desperately wants me to believe Isaiah's married. I just can't.

Isaiah's a pastor and he's just starting out. Even though his family has money, he's already told me his mother wasn't happy about him moving to Vegas. No way would she support him enough for him to be able to afford two residences.

Besides, I remember Mrs. Martin and there's no way she would accept Isaiah's wife working outside of the home. It's not done in her world.

"I don't believe you," I tell Harris.

"Doesn't make it untrue."

I stand up. I've had enough of Harris and his lies about Isaiah. "I have to go. There's a saleslady holding a dress for me."

"I have no reason to lie to you, Athena."

"Wrong. You have every reason to lie to me. Isaiah has no reason to lie to me." I stand up and leave the table before he can stop me. I start to walk back to the store, but out of the corner of my eye, I see the young girl and I change my mind.

The first time I tried to leave Mike, I told him about it.

It's late summer and I'm done. I'm not going to spend the rest of my life having sex with strangers and Mike's an idiot if he thinks I am. I pull a short black wig on. It won't disguise me, but for some reason it brings me a certain amount of security. He's standing silently in the doorway, watching me pack.

I don't know where I'm going. To be honest, as long as it's not here, I don't care where it is. I have two hundred dollars in my pocket. It won't last me long, but if I'm lucky I can find a cheap hotel room and maybe get a job sweeping floors or something. I'll do anything that doesn't involve sex or being naked.

It's embarrassing how little I have to pack in the battered suitcase. There'd probably be more, but I don't want most of what is in my apartment. I slam the top of the suitcase down and march past Mike. His smug expression pisses me off.

I'm early for the bus, which is a bad thing, because it gives me too much time to think. I keep doing the math in my head. I subtract how much the bus ticket will cost, and I'm afraid I won't have enough money to live.

What if I don't get a job as quickly as I think I will? How long can I afford to keep looking? Not nearly as long as I'd like. The doubts taunt me. I push them to the back of my mind because I know if I don't leave now, I won't ever do it. But they don't leave me alone.

No one will hire you with zero job experience for the last year.

When the money runs out, and it will, you'll be right back doing what you do best.

What kind of job do you think you're qualified for anyway?

The longer I sit, the louder they get, and the more I believe them.

I revise my plan. Maybe I'll just stay for another six months. No longer than a year. It'll give me time to save more money. I weigh it out in my head. Is it better to do another six months and guarantee I never have to sell myself again or leave now knowing I might have to?

When I leave, I'll never have sex for money again. Tears fill my eyes as I realize that means I should stay for now. The bus pulls up, and I feel sick because I'm not leaving on it. I tell myself it's better this way. This way I'll be financially secure when I do leave. And I will leave. I promise myself I will.

But something in my soul breaks, because I know that by deciding to stay, I'm choosing the life of a prostitute.

I don't watch as the bus drives off. It's enough that I smell the fumes from the bench I'm sitting on. Footsteps approach me. Slow. Even. Methodical. I brace myself for the inevitable.

"I knew you wouldn't leave me," Mike says.

Jackass.

"What are your plans now?" he asks.

"I'll keep on working for you." I mumble it, sickened to be saying the words.

"And what makes you think I want you back?"

My head snaps up, but he's completely serious, there's not a sign of teasing to be found.

"I thought.... I assumed... What?"

He's enjoying my discomfort, and even though I didn't think it possible, I hate him even more.

"Tell me why I should take you back when I have plenty of girls who never even think about leaving me." He towers over me.

"I don't have anywhere else to go."

"And I care because?"

Panic seeps into my body, and I don't know what I'll do if Mike doesn't take me back. "Please?"

"Not good enough."

I think about telling him I'll do anything, but I'm not that desperate. I don't want to imagine what his 'anything' would be, much less do it. I stare at the floor and his shiny leather shoes. I hate him so much.

"You still think you have a say in what you do," he says. "And that is very dangerous thinking. You eat because I choose to feed you. You sleep when I say you do. You have a roof over your head because I let you have one."

The man working the ticket counter picks that minute to come over to us. "Can I help you two with anything?"

"Athena?" Mike asks.

"No, I'm staying here," I manage to get out.

"Nothing for me," Mike says.

The gentleman tells us to let him know if we change our mind and walks back to his station.

"Unfortunately," Mike says. "We can't have this conversation here. Be in my office in fifteen minutes. And take that ridiculous wig off."

Later that night, I'm soaking in the tub back in my apartment. I'm sore all over, both inside and out. I would be crying, but I don't have any tears left. For a few seconds, the warmth of the water is so inviting, I imagine staying in it forever. I picture it in my head. It would be so easy. Slide into the water, hold my breath until I can't anymore. Surely, it wouldn't be that painful. Not in comparison to everything else.

The only thing that keeps me from doing it is hate. I hate Mike for what he's made me and what he makes me do. So instead of taking my life that night, I vow to one day take Mike's.

Chapter Fourteen

Whoever she is, she certainly isn't expecting a woman to sit next to her. She's been given a script and I'm nowhere in the act.

Too bad, I think toward the gentleman with her, but I keep my eyes away from him. *She's mine.*

I've been an actress for ten years, I can play this part, too.

I sit down beside her, cross my left leg over my right, and rub my calf. "Whew. I should not have worn these shoes."

Silence from the girl beside me. She probably thinks if she doesn't say anything, I'll go away faster. I plaster a smile on my face and look at her more fully. I was wrong earlier. She's nowhere near seventeen. She's fourteen, tops. Just the thought of what is planned for her makes me sick.

My left foot slides back to the floor and I try to make my smile warm and inviting. I don't think I do a good job.

"Shopping?" I ask, trying again for a response.

Her lower lip trembles. "No."

"Probably not here for the food." In the corner of my eye, I keep the man in my sight. He's taken a phone from his pocket and is texting someone.

"Not shopping. Not eating," I say. "That leaves meeting someone. Am I right?"

The lower lip tremble stops and determined resolve somehow slips into its place. "What's it to you?"

I shrug. Lean back into the bench. Make myself dissolve into nonchalant. "Just making conversation."

She risks a glance at black jean guy and straightens her shoulders. "Yeah, well, make it somewhere else."

"Just making conversation," I repeat, turning to her. "And passing out advice."

Her skin is smooth and flawless. There's a wariness in her eyes, but no sign of bitterness and rejection. Not yet, anyway. Her body is lithe and long. She's not yet grown into womanhood, but the blueprints are there. Under her adolescent skin, the woman she will become waits.

"I had to tell you," I start. Hard to believe I'd ever been that young. I clench my fist. So many years wasted. "Needed to tell you. He's not worth it."

She blushes, and I know I've guessed correctly. "I don't know what you're talking about," she says with a flip of her hair.

"He makes lots of promises. Tells you he loves you. That you have to prove your love." I probably haven't blushed in nine years. The life of a working girl sucks the blush right out of a person. It isn't too late for her yet. "But he's wrong. Love just is. It doesn't make demands."

She huffs, reaches down to her purse, pulls out a compact, and checks her lipstick.

"You see me as an obnoxious know-it-all," I say. She acts like she isn't listening, but I desperately hope some part of what I say sinks in. Would I have listened if someone had tried to give me advice ten years ago? I'm not sure. "And you're right. I'm a know-it-all because I've been where you are right now, and I made the wrong choice. Listen to me when I tell you it won't end with this one friend."

Beside me, her hand holding the compact trembles.

"I know his type, and he's got a long line of friends just waiting to have their turn at you." I cross my right leg over my left this time. Hopefully, the guy in black jeans thinks I'm a mall patron gabbing on and on about nothing. "Before you know it, you'll be dependent on him for everything. You won't breathe without thinking you need permission to use air."

She slowly puts the compact back in her purse and straightens her skirt.

"You can do anything. Be anything." I have never in my life wished for the ability to make a choice for someone. "Don't be me."

We sit in silence for long seconds. I roll my head around and around. This is me, just an achy shopper. I can be anyone. I am every woman. Or at least that's what I hope the man certain to be watching us thinks. I risk a peek: He was still texting. If I guess correctly, he probably has a group of five other girls, just like the one beside me, waiting and ready to do his every command.

I hate him.

"I know you won't leave him today," I finally say. "But I'm hopeful you'll at least think about it."

I probably haven't changed anything. She'll go through with what she came here to do, and she'll hate herself later. Maybe I've actually made it worse with my observations and advice.

Unfortunately, there isn't anything else I can do to help her. I'm useless. I can't offer her a viable alternative, or a place to stay. I stand up. "Chose wisely."

I almost miss the soft whisper behind me.

"Thank you."

If I were smart, I'd leave the food court and go back to buy the green dress like I told Harris I was doing. But I can't. I have to watch her: the possible Mrs. Isaiah Martin.

I move far enough away so I can see her without being seen myself. I try to act natural and not at all like I'm spying on a stranger. I can see Harris from my location, too. He's texting someone. He stands up when he finishes and looks around. Looking for me?

I move behind the directory I'm hiding myself with and wait. I count to fifty, and when I look again, he's gone. The supposed Mrs. Martin is still there. She's finishing up her lunch and telling her friend goodbye. The friend leaves, but Mrs. Martin's phone rings, so she sits back down and answers it. Whoever it is doesn't talk long, and in a few minutes, she pushes back from the table and rummages in her purse.

I shouldn't do it, but I step out from behind the directory, and when she leaves the food court heading out to the parking lot, I follow. I don't know what I hope to gain by doing so. Maybe I think Isaiah is outside.

She's moving fast. But the upside to that is she's not paying any attention to her surroundings. I lag behind her as she approaches her car, not wanting to be too obvious. She hops in an older model sedan that's a few rows away from the car Isaiah let me drive today.

I don't know what possesses me, but I jog to my car and start it up, determined to follow her. It's not hard. For all her urgency to make it to the car, she's a relatively slow driver. Very careful.

I'm a few cars behind her as we pull out of the parking lot and head south. I try to stay out of her view, just in case she is Isaiah's wife. I don't want her to recognize the car. She pulls onto a highway headed out of town. There's still a car between us, and for the first time I question my sanity in following her. What exactly do I expect to get out of this? That she's going to drive to her house and some man who isn't Isaiah is going to come out and greet her and I can return to the little condo I now consider home?

I snort at the impossibility.

More likely, she's probably headed somewhere that will prove nothing and I'll have wasted an entire afternoon. I won't have purchased any new clothes, and Isaiah will be perplexed when he gets home. I can imagine the conversation.

"You were following a woman you thought was my wife?"

He'll look at me like I've grown two heads, and we'll have a laugh over it. I'll tell him I knew there was no way he was married and he'll pretend to be angry I doubted him for even a second. He'll whisper that I'm nothing but trouble and to make it up to him I'll pour him some wine. Maybe when he's finished I'll pull him close and show him a different kind of trouble.

I'm so engrossed in my daydream, it's not until she turns onto a smaller road that I realize how far out of Vegas we are. Where the hell is she going? The traffic is sparse on this road. It's only the two of us. I let up on the gas, not wanting her to notice me.

It's when I drop back that I see it in the rearview mirror: a black SUV, careening down the road. I wonder where it's headed. The road continues its path into the nothingness of the desert, but I keep my eye on both the car before me and the one behind me. For some reason I can't put my finger on, the car following me seems off.

My suspicion is proven correct as we round a corner. There's nothing but empty desert on either side of me, and I think if I had to dump a body somewhere, this would be where I do it. No sooner do I think that than the car behind me speeds up. As it passes me, I see two men inside. Both are wearing ski masks.

It's one of those moments you don't really think is happening. Even as I stare at the retreating car's taillights, I'm thinking there's no way I just saw that. I wish I had a phone. But even thinking that, I know I wouldn't do anything if I had one. You can't very well call up the police because someone's driving around wearing ski masks.

I frown, because the car isn't passing the supposed Mrs. Martin. Instead, it's harassing her. Riding up on her bumper and then backing down again. *Now* I wish I had a phone. That sort of driving could get someone killed.

The lady driving is doing her best to hold the course steady. She's not speeding up or dropping back. She's not doing anything to antagonize the car behind her. I'm not sure what I'm going to do, but I speed up in an effort to get closer.

I'm closing the distance between myself and the SUV when its driver finally decides to pass. But as he pulls along beside her, I watch in horror as a hand holding a gun reaches out of the passenger side window and shoots.

I scream, helpless, as her car careens to the right and crashes into a cactus.

And then the gun is pointed at me. There's a terrific crash and everything goes dark.

Chapter Fifteen

The first thing I become aware of is the smell of gasoline. Raw. Suffocating. The taste trickles down my throat. Maybe I've died and this is hell. Certainly, I imagine, hell smells like gasoline.

I crack open one eye. Pain and light explode in front of me. I tentatively roll my head. This *is* hell. There's a fire somewhere nearby, and I'm still in the car. It takes everything I have to open the car door and crawl out.

My lungs are hungry for the fresh air outside the car, and I inhale in gulps. But I have to get away from the car. I don't know if it's going to blow up or if that only happens in the movies.

In front of me is the strange lady's car, and I think I see something moving inside. I half walk, half crawl to the door. I have a faint memory of a gun, but maybe that was a dream.

I reach the door and pull myself up so I can see inside. She's been shot. There's a horrific wound in her shoulder that looks too close to her heart. She turns her head to look at me and moans.

I try to open the door, but it was damaged in the crash and won't budge.

"Help... me..." the lady says.

"I'm trying. It's stuck."

I give it a hard jerk, and though it feels like my arm's going to be ripped out of its socket, I get it open. She's already undone her seatbelt somehow, so I ease my arms around her and help her out as best I can.

My strength is shot, and I barely get her out before we both fall to the ground. I grit my teeth and move her into a more comfortable position, but I know I'm not doing any good. The blood from her wound has already pooled in the dirt, and I can't comprehend how she's still alive.

Her soft moan proves she is, though. At least for now.

I fall to my knees beside her. I'd thought I could do something, anything to help her, but there's nothing I can do. She's alive for the moment, however, even someone with my lack of medical knowledge knows she won't be for long.

I take her hand, delicate, fragile in my own, and softly stroke her skin. Black soot and red blood swirls together.

"It hurts," she whispers. "So much."

"I'm sorry." Tears rolls down my cheeks, fall, and mix with the sludge covering her as I cry for this woman I don't know. I brush my fingers across her forehead. She's ice. "Just hang on. It'll be okay."

We both know it's a lie.

"Help will be here soon." Surely someone has spotted the fire and called someone.

The fire from my car burns steadily. It's inching toward us, but I can't move her.

I whisper nonsensical words to her instead. I murmur little phrases of nothing in particular. I want to somehow take away the pain and hurt, but I know I fail completely.

Her body jerks upwards and she gasps.

"I'm sorry," I stroke her hand once more. "So sorry."

"Oh."

I glance to her face and her eyes blaze with a clarity that wasn't there seconds before. She's focused on something behind me.

I fear it's the person who shot her, but I look over my should and there's no one there. "Are you okay?" A stupid question, but the only one I can form.

"He's coming."

I pat her hand. "I'm sure they're on their way."

"Him."

"Yes." I don't seem to be able to disagree with her. Maybe I should look for her cell phone. I glance around, maybe it's in her purse. Nothing.

"Let me call someone," I offer. "Just need to find your phone."

"He's coming."

I don't see a purse anywhere. Either it's still in the hump of scrambled metal that's now the remains of her car, or it had been thrown out during the crash.

"I don't know where your phone is. I can't call anyone. I'm sure the police are coming." I'm such a failure. "I don't know anything."

Her lips curl into a calm and joyous smile. "Not the police."

Her chest rises, but doesn't fall.

Sirens sound in the distance.

I don't see her again. While I'm in the emergency room, I try asking the nurses around me about her, but they don't say anything. I'm not too surprised; in the controlled chaos of the environment, there's really not much time for them to sit around and chit chat. Not to mention, I'm sure it's against the law for them to divulge any of that information to me.

I'm stuck in the ER for hours. I tell anyone who comes by that I'm fine and I want to leave, but I'm told I have to stay overnight for observation. My protests that there's nothing wrong with me falls on deaf ears. I try not to think about how much the stay in the hospital is going to cost. Hopefully, the administration has some plan in place for those of us without insurance.

I don't like being in the hospital. I know no one likes it, but for me, I feel exposed. There's security in place, but for the most part, anyone who wants to can come in. I hope beyond hope Mike doesn't find out I'm here. I'll be an easy target until I get out.

It's only when I'm finally in my room and the nurse's aide is checking my blood pressure that I finally get answers.

"The lady I was brought in with," I say then stop. I don't know her name. I don't know anything about her other than what Harris told me, and I'm not certain he was being honest.

"Jane Doe?" the aide asks. "Poor thing. You don't know her do you?"

I shake my head.

"I heard the police are trying to find out who she is. She didn't have any identification on her."

That doesn't make sense. I think back to the food court. I know she had a purse. She dug into it to find her keys.

"What about her purse?" I ask.

"They didn't find one. Or at least that's what I heard."

My head was already hurting, and now it's pounding. I can't tell her she had a purse in the food court because that'll give away the fact I was following her. My memories of the crash are too fuzzy, I can't remember exactly what happened.

My entire body suddenly freezes.

"Ma'am," the aid says. "Are you okay?"

"They were there," I mumble.

"Honey you need to calm down. Your pulse is racing, and your blood pressure's climbing."

Whoever shot her came back to the scene and took her purse. It's the only thing that makes sense. Which means they know who I am.

She's adjusting the cuff on my arm to take another reading, but stop her. "I have to leave."

"Not until they release you."

"No, I have to leave now."

"Calm down. You need to rest."

I'm too weak to struggle with her, and she's not listening to me. My repetitive, "Please" isn't doing any good. In fact, it appears to have the opposite effect. She's concerned with my blood pressure reading, but in all honesty, all her repetitions of "Calm down" over and over again are just making my discomfort grow. She's not listening, and those men who killed that woman and tried to kill me are out there, and so is Mike.

My eyelids grow heavy and I glare at the aid. "What did you give me?"

"Something to help you rest."

"Don't want to," I start, but the drugs take over and I'm out before I finish the sentence.

It's dark when I wake up. The room is still, but something's off, I sense it as soon as I open my eyes. I close them again, because I know what it is. Someone's in the room with me.

"I know you're awake."

Harris.

At least it's him and not Mike. "Why didn't you kill me when I was asleep? Will waiting until I'm awake give you some sort of thrill?" It's big talk for someone hooked up to an IV and wearing a backless gown.

"I wanted to make sure you were safe." His voice is expressionless when he talks.

I don't say anything else. The pieces are starting to fall into place. Harris found me at the food court. He set up the lunch between the two women, and when the one left, he called the one he said was Isaiah's wife. The crash was arranged, because he knew I'd follow her.

In the dark, his presence grows stronger. He was in the car. That's why he wore a mask, so I wouldn't recognize him. And after the crash, while I was still out, he stole the lady's purse. Because *he knew* she wasn't Isaiah's wife.

"Get out of my room," I say.

"Athena, listen."

"Don't *listen* me. I know what you're doing. You're keeping guard until Mike gets back. I'm not going back to him."

"I'm not —"

"You've been stalking me for days. How else would you know I'm here?'

"I'm your only chance to get out of this alive."

"Why would you want to keep me alive? Because I'm worth more to Mike that way? Screw you. Get out of my room."

"What do I have to do to get you to believe me?"

"There's nothing you can do. I'm never going to believe you. That woman wasn't Isaiah's wife. They're calling her Jane Doe."

"Because they took her ID."

It's so close to what I'd imagined, my blood runs cold. "Get out. Or I call for help."

"Damn it, Athena."

"Now."

He doesn't argue further. I hear the chair moan as he stands up. For a second, I think he's going to say something else, but he doesn't. His footsteps echo softly as he walks out.

My head is still fuzzy from the drugs they gave me, yet even with all that, there is one clear thought running through my head. *Get out. Get out now.*

I'm not connected to the IV any longer; they must have taken that out while I was out of it. Can I simply get out of bed and walk out the door? Possibly, but I don't have any clothes. I'm going to have to find some though, it's imperative I leave the hospital tonight. I know that if I'm still here in the morning, I'm as good as dead.

And I need to warn Vicki. I'm not sure what she tried to tell me before I went to Theo's room, but she knew something. I need to tell her she was right. Maybe, just maybe, she has some money, and we can run away together. It'll be safer with two people.

The downside is I'll have to go back to our apartment complex, and Mike or one of his henchmen might be there. That's another reason I need to leave tonight. If he thinks I'm still in the hospital, maybe he won't be waiting for me.

I doubt there are any spare clothes in the room I'm in, and if I were to bet, the ones I had on in the crash were discarded. Damn it. I refuse to let a little thing like a lack of clothes keep me from leaving.

I sit up, fighting the dizzy feeling that tries to overtake me when I do so. Ever so slowly, I swing my legs over the edge of the bed, and for a few seconds I stay there.

You can do this. You can do this. You can do this.

Eventually it becomes:

You have to do this. You have to do this. You have to do this.

My legs wobble when I slide off the bed, but I hold on to the rail long enough to steady myself. Damn it all. I can barely stand, how do I think I'm going to leave without drawing attention to myself?

I grit my teeth, scoop up my shoes, and shuffle toward the door. Easing it open, just a crack, I peek into the corridor. It's empty. Not only that, but there's a laundry cart across the hall from me. Housekeeping is cleaning out a recently vacated room. All I have to do is find something clean to wear.

I hear someone humming from inside the room, and I decide I'm good as long as the sound doesn't come any closer. My heart pounds as I slide toward the cart. There's a stack of scrubs folded on a shelf. I snatch them and duck into a nearby ladies room.

The restroom is deserted this time of night and I close the door and lean against it, catching my breath. The accident took more out of me than I thought. But to survive, I must get out of Vegas.

When I feel strong enough, I switch clothes and throw the hospital gown in the trash. Maybe no one will see it before I'm able to leave. I bend over to slip my shoes on and something is sticking out. It's two twenty-dollar bills and a handful of ones. There's also a note.

Sorry, it's all I had.

The only person it could have been was Harris, and my mind tries to wrap itself around that. I don't want to take his money, but it'll pay for cab fare to Vicki's. I count out the ones. I need an accurate total so I can pay him back.

It's easier than I would have thought possible to leave the hospital. With the scrubs on, I blend in, and no one looks twice at me. Once I hail a cab, I lean back into the seat, but I can't rejoice in my freedom just yet. Maybe when I get out of this God-awful city.

The apartment complex appears quiet as we approach. I tell the cab driver to stop before we get to it and let me out. On the off chance someone's watching, I don't want them to see the cab.

My heart pounds so hard when I step out of the cab, I'm surprised I can't hear the sound echoing. Otherwise, it's eerily quiet. Both my apartment and Vicki's are dark. Even so, I plan to look over everything before going inside.

Once I'm in the parking lot, I hide between the cars, scoping out the next set I plan to hide between and looking around for any signs of movement or people waiting inside cars. My eyes have adjusted to the low light, and I dart between an SUV and pick-up truck. After scanning the empty area between me and Vicki's door, I move as quickly as my legs will let me.

Seconds before I reach her door, something jumps out of the shadows. I'm barely able to muffle my scream, but I manage to do it, and I breath a sigh of relief it's only a cat.

I lean against her door and wait for my heart to slow. Fortunately, everything appears calm and normal.

I have no way of knowing what time it is. It's dark inside her apartment. I don't know if she's out or if she's asleep. If she's out, I'm not sticking around. Each minute I'm here is a risk and though I want to warn her, it's not a risk I'll allow myself to take twice.

I take a deep breath and knock softly. "Vicki," I whisper. "It's me. Open up."

I put my ear against the door, but I don't hear anything. *Damn it.* I really wanted her to be home. I knock harder this time. Maybe she's sleeping. "Vicki."

This time I hear footsteps and I exhale a shaky breath. *Yes.*

The door opens and before I can scream, Harris has his arms around me with his hand over my mouth and he's whispering in my ear. "Shut up and keep it down."

It's sad how little effort he has to exert to pick me up and bring me inside. He puts me on my feet and turns on the light.

"Welcome back home, Athena."

Mike is sitting in Vicki's living room.

Chapter Sixteen

I want to call Harris a fucking traitor, but I'm so shaken at seeing both men in Vicki's apartment, I can't find the words. Behind me, Harris's grip is strong and keeps me from running.

"Harris didn't think you'd come back," Mike says. "Why that is, I'm not sure. I told him you may not go to your place, but I figured you'd stop by to see Vicki and we just needed to be patient."

I look around the apartment, trying to find something, anything, that can be used as a weapon. From what I can tell, my two choices are a letter opener and a beer bottle. I doubt I have the strength to break the beer bottle, so it's going to have to be the letter opener. It's to my right, on a table by the door. It'll be a stretch, but if I can move fast enough, I might just be able to grab it and stab at least one of the men. I'll probably aim for Mike.

He stands up and smirks at my attire. "Hospital scrubs? Really?"

I glare at him, trying to keep his attention so he doesn't see the letter opener or my fingers inching toward it. Harris is standing behind me, I can't tell what he's focusing on, but if luck's on my side, he's not paying attention to my hand.

"Harris obviously thinks you're much smarter than you are," Mike says. "Why you're not fifty miles away by now, I don't know." He reaches a hand out to touch my cheek. I steel myself so I don't flinch. He's pressing a bruise and it hurts like hell. "Of course, you're not in the best shape to travel right now, are you?"

I keep my eyes on him, but don't say anything. I probably won't be able to stand much longer. I'm far too weak, but I can't let them see that. And more than anything, I have to get that letter opener.

"Nothing to say?" Mike asks. "I'm not sure what to do with you. In all honesty, it would have been easier if you stayed away. But you're here, so we have to deal with you."

Don't show fear. Don't show fear. Don't show fear.

I try to remember if he had anything in his hands when he first stood up. I'm too tired. I can't recall. And I'm not about to drop my eyes to check. My fingers move another inch toward the letter opener.

"You're not much use to me," he continues. "You've been nothing but a bunch of bruises for the last week. I can't put you to work looking like you are."

There's an uncanny silence in the room. It occurs to me: The letter opener is probably my only hope to get out of this apartment alive. I take a deep breath and will my heart to slow down.

"Theo was quite upset you left so quickly and without saying anything. You've probably guessed already, but I sent Vicki to take your place." His lips curl up into an ugly grin. "He wasn't very nice to her from what I heard. Think he probably took some of his anger at you on her."

Guilt floods me, because not once since being pulled into her apartment have I actually wondered where Vicki is. Then an entirely new kind of guilt hits me: She's being hurt because of me. She tried to warn me, and I didn't listen. What if I'd listened to her that day instead of being so determined to get to Theo's? Maybe we'd both be safe.

But I tell myself I can't dwell on the what ifs, I have to focus on staying upright and reaching the letter opener. There'll be time for what ifs later. I think briefly about asking to take her place, but I'm not going to. Doing so would show emotion, and I never show emotion to Mike if I can help it.

"I could send you back to Theo," Mike says in echo to my thoughts. "At least that would get you out of my hair. If I'm lucky, maybe he'll keep you out of my hair forever."

In my mind, I plan my next movements. It's my one chance, and I'm going to take it.

"What do you think about that?" Mike asks.

I spit at him and lunge for the letter opener at the same time. If anyone other than Harris held me, I probably would have made it. Unfortunately, Harris is onto my plan and he takes my wrist.

"Drop it."

I try to stab Harris with my makeshift weapon, but he's too strong. Before me, Mike is wiping his eyes and my blood runs cold at the look in them.

"That was a mistake." He plucks the letter opener from my hand with such ease I could cry. "A letter opener? Really, Athena?"

"It would have worked if this Neanderthal hadn't been holding me." I've just lost my one shot at getting away. They're probably going to kill me anyway. I don't see any reason not to share everything on my mind.

Mike moves so fast, I'm not sure I blink before I realize he has a gun pointed at me. "Tell me why I shouldn't shoot you now."

I take a deep breath to scream, but Harris smacks his hand over my mouth. My skin breaks out in a cold sweat, and I can't keep my eyes off the gun.

"Mike. Stop." Harris's voice is deep in my ear.

"Stay out of this," Mike says, not moving his gaze from my face.

"You brought me here for a reason. I don't think you want me to stay out of this."

"What's she to you?"

"Nothing. She's nothing to me. But that doesn't mean I want her dead."

"You getting soft, Harris?"

"I think killing her is more work than we need right now."

Mike slowly lowers the gun. "True, and if she's alive, she'll be thinking about what's happening to Vicki."

I'm not able to stop my flinch at his words. He sees, of course, and he obviously likes that.

"But I still don't know what to do with her. She's too much trouble to keep here."

I've been standing too long and have had too many endorphins running through my body. My legs aren't going to keep me upright much longer.

The odd thought strikes me that I can't remember when I last ate anything. No wonder I'm swaying and everything seems so surreal.

My body decides it's taking too much energy to stay upright, and my knees buckle. Only Harris's arms keep me from hitting the floor. My vision starts to fade.

"Worthless," Mike says, a look of disgust on his face. "She's no good to me in this shape, and she can't be out anymore. I need working girls, I'm not running a fucking hospital. Speaking of which," he prods me with his foot, "If you think I'm paying that hospital bill, you're sorely mistaken."

I try to say something, but nothing comes out. The darkness is taking over.

"Let me have her," Harris says.

Those are the last words I hear before the dark wins completely.

"Athena." Mike has stopped by my apartment. It's not common for him to do so these days. I've been with him eight years, and I typically do my best to stay away from him. It's probably been a year since he last decided to grace my apartment with his presence.

And today he's not alone.

I don't picture the guy with him as a client or customer. After so many years, I'm usually able to pick those men out. Normally, something in their eyes give them away, or the lift of their mouth does. This guy, though, I don't know what he's doing with Mike.

"This is Harris," Mike says, and the new guy nods.

He's not unpleasant to look at. In fact, many would probably call him good-looking. Unfortunately, he's obviously friends with Mike, so that makes him ugly as hell to me. I try to keep my eyes on Mike, but something about Harris makes that difficult.

It's more than his looks; it's the way he holds himself. His demeanor. He has a bold confidence that doesn't seem to be intimidated by Mike. It's nothing I've seen before, and I wish I had that confidence.

"Harris, this is Athena. She's very special to me."

I try not to roll my eyes at Mike's statement.

"Hello, Harris," I say and nod. I don't touch men as a rule if I don't have to.

"Goddess of wisdom?" Harris asks, his voice friendly.

"Ironic, right?" I reply. "If my parents only knew."

I kick myself for being so flippant. I know better than to be sucked in by a friendly voice and a pleasant looking exterior. But Harris is grinning. Wisely, he doesn't mention my parents.

"I wanted you to meet him," Mike says as if we didn't say anything. "He's going to be working with me now. He'll be my second in command."

"Huh, that's too bad," I say, looking straight at Harris. "Now I can't like you."

Mike looks like he's going to hit me, but Harris laughs and slaps him on the shoulder. "I see why she's so special to you."

He's laughing, but it's true. Besides, he's new. He won't be laughing for very long.

When I wake up, I'm in a car. It catches me off guard, because I thought I'd already be dead or at least halfway there. I don't open my eyes just yet. I want to gather as much information as possible without letting whoever's around know I'm awake.

I'm reclining, which means I'm probably in the passenger seat. We're moving rather fast, so I'm guessing we're not in the city. We must be on a highway. I don't feel anything around my arms or legs. Normally, I'd feel relieved that whoever I'm with didn't feel the need to tie me up, but I'm in such bad shape, they probably knew they didn't need to.

My left leg is asleep. I stretch it and, fuck, it hurts like hell.I gasp.

"Awake?"

It's Harris.

I don't answer him at first. I'm trying to decide how I feel that it's him I'm in the car with. While it's better than being in the car with Mike, it's not that much better. He is Mike's second in command, after all. Of course, having said that, Harris has never physically hurt me, and he did stop Mike from shooting me. I wonder why?

"Why am I here?" I ask.

"We're going to my house."

"Why?"

"Because Mike is letting me have you until he decides what to do with you."

He's letting Harris have me. It sickens me. Being away from my former occupation, even for a few days, has impacted me. I'm already getting addicted to the moments I've had of a normal lifestyle. One where I'm not giving myself away. I don't think I can go back to it. Especially with Harris.

"Figures," I say.

"What?" he asks.

I adjust my seat so I'm sitting upright, and I wince in pain.

"I'll give you something to help the aches and pains when we get to my house. Now tell me what you meant by saying it figures."

It's easy to be myself around Harris and tell him exactly how I feel. I don't like it, and I can't explain it, but that's how it is. I try to tell myself he's a dangerous man, but it doesn't work.

"It always seems to me that you try to separate yourself from Mike. That doesn't make sense, because you work so closely with him, but that's the impression I get." I peek over at him, and his lips are pulled down in a frown. "Yet in the end, you're just like everyone else."

"What does that mean?"

"It means that when it all boils down, you're really just biding your time until you can have a piece of me, too."

His frown deepens, and he slows the car down. I look around franticly; we're in the middle of nowhere. "Why are you slowing down?"

He's silent as he pulls well off the road and comes to a stop. In that moment, I know I've pushed him too far.

"I'm sorry. I didn't mean it like that. I'll shut up. Please don't."

When the car comes to a stop and he turns to face me, it isn't anger in his eyes, but shock. "Damn it, Athena. What the hell do you think I'm going to do?"

"You were pulling off the road because I said something rude and snarky. What do you think I believed was going to happen?"

"You thought I was going to hit you?"

"Or worse."

He sighs. "I pulled off the road because I wanted to give you my full attention, and I can't do that and drive at the same time."

"Oh." I should feel guilty for thinking Harris would treat me like that, but I don't. When you've been around as many men as I have, you realize that even the nicest ones have secrets. And you should never underestimate the strength a man has, because some of the strongest men I've met are small. Although no one would ever call Harris small.

"To answer your question, Mike has assigned me as your keeper until he can find you a partner."

"Partner?" I've know Mike for over ten years. There is no way he's looking for a *partner* for me. "I don't believe you."

"You've said that a lot to me lately." He almost smiles. "I wouldn't know what to think if you actually did believe me."

"No, I believe he assigned me to you, but I don't buy the line about a partner." I raise an eyebrow. "When you say *gave....*"

For the first time since I woke up in his car, Harris isn't smiling. His face contorts into an expression of disgust. "His exact words were, 'Do what you want with her, but try to keep her alive.'"

Try to keep her alive.

My stomach revolts even though it's empty, and I dry heave. That one phrase echoes in my head. *Try to keep her alive. Try to keep her alive.*

"Athena." Harris's voice is faint. "You're okay. Take deep breaths."

But I'm not. I'm not okay. Mike took away my ability to be okay years ago, and no matter how hard I try, I never seem to be able to take it back.

"Let me leave," I say in-between heaves. "Please."

"I can't do that."

Right. Because even though he acts nice, he reports to Mike. I'll do well to remember that.

"Don't look at me like that," he says. "Do you know how dangerous it'd be for me to let you go?"

I'm doing this for your own good. Fuck, it's almost like Mike told him exactly what to say. My life is one horribly messed up glob of lies that someone tried to dust off and make look pretty, but the sad truth is, at the end of the day, it's still a glob of lies. I'm so tired of lies.

Just this once.

It won't matter.

You'll love it.

I'm only looking out for you.

It'll be okay.

"One day," I tell Harris. "I'm getting out and I'm going somewhere where I get to decide what's best for me."

He's nodding. "I understand your desire for that. Now's not the time."

For a minute, I get the impression there's a hidden meaning behind his words. Almost as if he's trying to tell me something. I tilt my head. He really does have pretty eyes. And right now they're begging me to understand.

"Who are you, Harris?" I say.

He doesn't flinch. "I don't know what you mean."

"Let's start with your last name."

"My last name is Harris."

"Your name's Harris Harris?" I can't help it; I laugh. "How did you manage to piss your mom off so badly before you were born?"

He starts the car again and pulls onto the highway. "I didn't piss my mom off before I was born. Harris isn't my first name."

"What's your first name?"

"Caden."

I wrinkle my nose. "Harris Harris is better."

"I'll tell my mom."

We're a few miles down the road before I realize I'm smiling.

You are so fucked up. You shouldn't be comfortable with this man.

But my smile doesn't go away.

He drives us to a house about fifteen minutes outside of Vegas. The home he pulls up to is larger than I would have imagined a bachelor living in. And though it's not isolated, his neighbors aren't so close he can see what they're eating for dinner by looking out his window.

"Big place for a guy living by himself." As soon as the words come out of my mouth I realize I have no way of being certain he actually lives by himself. For all I know, he could be married with five kids.

But he replies simply, "I like my space."

I'm more sore than I thought and it hurts like hell to climb out of the car. Harris is by my side in a flash after hearing my moan.

"You should have waited for me."

"I'm perfectly capable of getting out of a car," I snap back.

He takes my attitude in stride, neither getting angry or coddling me. "I have some of your clothes in the trunk— "

"Don't want them." I start to hobble to the door.

"You have to wear something."

I stop and turn around. "Caden Harris, I've had a woman die in my arms. I've almost been killed. I haven't had anything to eat in I don't know how long. I've been this close to escaping from the jackass who's owned me for the last ten years and not long ago I was given to a man with instructions to do what he wanted to with me as long as he kept, rather *tried* to keep, me alive. Shove the clothes up your ass. I'll go naked before I wear them."

His eyes crinkle at the corners, and he's trying hard not to laugh. "Do you want the toothbrush, or should I shove it up my ass, too?"

There's no way to answer him, so I head back to the door and wait for him to unlock it.

He closes the trunk, wisely leaving the clothes where they are. "There's a public nudity restriction in my homeowners agreement, so wrap a towel or something around you before heading outside. Deal?"

"Deal," I say as he opens the door and waves me inside.

He leads me down a short hallway into a spacious kitchen. "I'll give you the grand tour later, but right now you need something for the pain and food."

My stomach rumbles at the thought of eating. Harris opens the nearby pantry and starts pulling things out. "Peanut butter and jelly sound good? It's quick and easy to make, plus it has protein."

"Sounds delightful."

He waves toward a table in front of a bay window. "Go sit down and let me get this ready."

I don't need to be told twice. I sit down and watch him work. He's making himself a sandwich, too.

"Milk or something else?" he asks.

"Milk's fine."

Minutes later, he places the sandwich, milk, and two pills in front of me before taking his seat across from me. I raise my eyebrow at the pills.

"Ibuprofen," he says.

I swallow them before taking a bite of the sandwich. "Oh my, God," I say after my first bite. "This is the best peanut butter and jelly sandwich I've ever had."

"Or else you were starving."

"That, too," I say around my second bite.

He's quiet as I eat, and I appreciate the silence. As my belly is filled, my eyes grow more and more heavy. I'm surprised I'm not snoring by the time I pop the last bit of bread in my mouth. Harris has been watching me carefully, and when I finish, he stands up.

"We need to talk, but you need to sleep first," he says.

I yawn, but push back from the table and follow him down a hall. He points to a bedroom. "That's my room. You'll be here," he indicates an adjacent room.

Well, that answered one of my questions. I wouldn't be sleeping in the same bed as he did. Which didn't mean he wouldn't expect sex at some point. Matter of fact, I'd be willing to bet he would want to sleep with me. Probably not now.

"A shower." It hits me. I'd been so caught up in food, I forgot how rank I probably was.

He looks over me in assessment. "You're barely able to keep your eyes open. I don't think you and water would be good now."

I yawn again. This time, bigger than the one in the kitchen. "You're right."

"I know I am." He doesn't step inside the bedroom he's declared mine. "Sleep now. When you wake up, you can take a shower and we'll talk."

He may be talking more, I'm not sure. My mind is totally not paying attention to him anymore. My focus is on the bed in front of me. It looks so inviting. I'll sleep on top of the covers; that way I won't get them smelly.

Harris says something from the doorway.

"What?" I ask.

"Come find me after you wake up and shower."

"Yes," I say, climbing up on the bed. "Sometime next year."

He chuckles and closes the door.

I'm in a dark room. Either that or I'm blindfolded. I can't tell which. I'm also naked. It's cold in the room and wish I had something to cover my body.

"Absolute perfection," a strange voice says.

I turn my head in the direction it's coming from, but there's nothing there. Must be a blindfold on me.

"She is," a voice says that is eerily familiar. "Would you like to try her out?"

Someone unzips his pants. "How good is she at sucking dick?"

"She's superb. But don't you want her tight ass?"

"Maybe. I prefer my fucks to be intelligent as well as easy on the eye, though. Did she go to college?"

"She didn't finish high school. Now, this one over here..."

His voice grows softer as they move away from me. I have a feeling I just failed something, but I don't know what it is. I'm not sure where I am or who's with me, and with my blindfold, I can't get a good feel of my surroundings. The air around me moves and it suddenly gets colder.

"No one wants you."

Mike! I struggle to move, but I can't get my limbs to cooperate.

"Tsk, tsk, tsk. You ever wonder why you never see an old whore?"

I must be tied to something. I'm getting nowhere and nothing comes out of my mouth when I try to scream.

You don't see one because there aren't any." He draws closer to me. "And I think you're old as you're going to get."

There's something covering my face. Pressing. It's a pillow and it's getting harder and harder to breathe. I try to turn my head, but he's too strong. My limbs flail uselessly. I can't breathe. My lungs burn for air.

"Athena," Harris's voice pulls me from the darkness. "Athena!"

I suck in a deep breath and open my eyes.

"Are you okay?" Harris's normally jovial eyes are filled with concern. "You had a bad dream."

"I couldn't breathe." The dream had seemed so lifelike that my lungs still ached.

"That's probably because Munchkin decided your head made a good pillow."

For the first time I see the large white cat beside me. "Munchkin?"

"He was the runt of the litter."

"He's part horse."

The large ball of fur must sense that we're discussing him. He rolls onto this back and Harris responds by rubbing his belly. "I think he's mostly dog."

Munchkin is purring. I reach for him and run my fingers over his soft fur. "I always wanted a pet. A dog or a cat."

For a few minutes we're silent, both of us rubbing Munchkin's belly. It's crazy how different my life has been the last few weeks compared to what it was for the last ten years. Sitting on a strange bed, in a strange house, petting a strange cat, doesn't feel all that strange for some reason. I like it, but, then again, I look over to Harris. I shouldn't like it.

Sure he appears nice enough, but they all do in the beginning. I can't forget that even though this is a nice-looking house and there aren't bars and gates, it's still a prison. I can't just decide to leave and walk out the door.

And no matter how good-looking he is, how nice, and how much he smiles, Caden Harris is still my jailer.

I pull away from Munchkin. "What did you want to talk about? I'm rested and not hungry. I'll shower after."

If Harris notes a change in my attitude, it doesn't show. He says, "Okay, let's go into the living room," and scoops the monster cat off the bed. I follow him.

Like the other parts of the house I've seen, the living room is decorated in American bachelor fashion: big screen TV, leather sofa and recliners, and a desk in the corner with more electronic devices than most office supply stores have.

When he sits down on one end of the sofa and faces me, all traces of humor have left his expression.

"I made a deal with Mike to get you out of there. I can't tell you everything, but what I do tell you is true. Do you trust me?"

I almost say 'yes'. It's the answer he's looking for, the one he wants. But I can't do it.

"No," I finally reply.

"I can't say I blame you," he says. "I'm not sure I'd trust me either."

"What kind of a deal did you make with Mike?"

"I was able to bring you here because I told him I'd see to it that you were prepared for your next assignment."

"Which is?"

He shakes his head. "I can't tell you that right now."

"This is why I can't trust you."

"I know, and I'm sorry, but there are things I can't tell you right now."

The leather of the sofa is cool against my fingers. It feels good against my heated flesh. "This isn't over, is it?"

"Not by a long shot, I'm afraid. I did get his permission to stay at home for the foreseeable future."

Which meant he would always be around. I'd be lying if I said the thought hadn't crossed my mind to simply leave the house when he went into work. Another useless plan shot to hell.

"The other thing," he starts, and I already dread what the other thing is. "Mike's letting me stay here and not be at the office with him because he's set up video conferences to monitor your progress with me."

What the ever-loving fuck? "Say that again."

"He's going to monitor your progress via webcam and let me work from home. I'll let you know when to expect them so you won't be caught off guard."

"Mike won't be here?" I ask

"Not unless he thinks I'm a miserable failure based on what he sees on the video."

I inhale deeply and ask the question weighing heavy on my mind. "What happens to me after he's satisfied with my progress?"

"Athena, look at me." His blue eyes beseech me, and when I look into them, I see the truth I saw long years ago when we first met. He's not like the others. "I need you to trust me on this. I don't know the timing and I don't know exactly when Mike will want you for your next assignment, but for right now, you're safe."

"I'm trapped here. That' s not safe. I can't leave when I want or go where I want. I can't even —"

"Do you want to live?"

His question knocks the wind out of me. "Yes."

"Then I need you to do the hardest thing you've ever done. I need you to trust me."

He may as well have asked for the moon. That's just about as likely to happen.

I feel even more human after my shower: clean, refreshed, and with a full belly, plus I'm not as achy as I was before. I hurry down the stairs and see that Harris is outside on his back deck. I pour myself a glass of water in the kitchen and join him.

He looks up at my arrival. "Feel better?"

"Much," I say, taking a seat in the chair beside him. "I did some thinking."

He doesn't reply but waits for me to continue.

"I thought about what you said earlier. I'm still not happy about being here, but you've never done anything to hurt me, so I'm going to trust you."

"Thank you, but you don't have to make it sound like a fate worse than death."

"I'm not. I know death would be worse." I glance sideways at him. "With you, death is only a possibility, not a certainty. That makes it marginally better."

He looks at me in shock.

"I'm kidding." I say. "I think."

He chuckles to himself. "You're an amazing woman, did you know that, Athena?"

No one has ever called me that before and I'm momentarily stunned. "No," I whisper.

"You have a quiet strength about you."

"I'm not so quiet."

He ignores my comment. "And you're a survivor. Look at everything you've been through."

I can't help the snort that comes out of my mouth. "I'm no such thing. You have to remember, I wasn't forced into this profession. I choose it."

"How old were you?"

"Sixteen."

"Sounds to me like your choice was do it or die. That's not picking a career path; that's survival."

"The only thing I'm surviving is life."

"Life isn't meant to be survived, it's meant to be delighted in."

"Is that what you do?" I ask. "You delight in life? Seriously? Working for Mike?"

A haunted expression crosses his face, and I know no matter what he says, he isn't always delighting in life. Sometimes, he's just surviving it as well.

"Then maybe," I say. "Maybe I'm just surviving my bad decisions."

"Athena."

I slowly turn my head and look into his captivating blue eyes. All earlier signs of playfulness are gone, replaced by an unwavering seriousness, but still somehow underscored by his usual gentleness.

"We call it 'the past' for a reason," he says. "Let it go."

"It's not a button you can just press. It's there. In my head. It's me." I run my fingers through my own hair. "I see it when I look in the mirror. I hear it at night when it's quiet. I feel it. Always."

"And it'll always be there. Our past is part of who we are, but it doesn't control our future. It doesn't dictate who we become."

He's right, and my head understands, but how did one go about convincing the heart?

"If you'd let me go, I could start over easy," I say.

He shakes his head. "That's the thing about pasts: You can't run from them. You have to accept them as part of you and move on."

"You act like you you're talking from experience," I say. "What could you possibly know about pasts? What deep dark secrets have you accepted?"

A haunted look flickers across his expression. He works for Mike, I tell myself. That in and of itself is dark enough. There's no telling what he's been a part of in the last few years.

"There are parts of me so deep and dark, I didn't visit them for the longest time." His voice is low and tinged with sadness. "But it was only by visiting them, looking them full in the face and accepting they would *never go away,* that I was able to move past them."

His exposed grief at whatever it was he accepted leaves a lump in my throat.

"Hello, my name is Athena and I'm a hooker?" I ask in a halfhearted way to lighten the mood and bring back the teasing. I can't handle deep and dark right now. I just can't. I can barely handle my own past, I can't take on his, too.

His mouth quirks up at the corner. "It's been known to work."

"First support group I find for whores, I'll join, then." I take a sip of water.

A strong hand stops mine. "Look at me. Stop thinking about yourself as some thing. As some commodity to be bartered and sold. Rented by the hour." His hand slides up, and he cups my face. "You are a beautiful, strong woman. What'll it take to make you believe it?"

"I don't know," I said, mesmerized by this change, this new, almost raw, Harris.

For several long minutes, we sit still. I am acutely aware of him. His presence almost overwhelms me, and I realize with a shock I'm not flinching at his touch. The fingers on my face are gentle and spark something inside me. I tremble at this new feeling.

"I'm sorry." He drops his hand, and though he probably thinks I didn't like his touch, I don't correct him. It's much easier that way, to pretend I didn't like it when in actuality, I wanted more.

"I should probably go get dinner started. You're welcome to stay out here if you'd like."

I find it rather lonely without Harris. His backyard is nice and fenced in. I can easily picture a dog running around with Harris playing catch. I hear something from inside the house and I realize Harris is humming.

Fascinated, I go back into the house. He's in the kitchen making some sort of pasta. When was the last time I heard someone hum? He looks up, catching me watching him, and gives me a wink. I hastily glance away, and then I chide myself for being childish.

To stop myself from doing it again, I take a tour of his living room. Plus, I want to see if I can find out any more information about him. The only personal touch I can find is a set of photos on an end table. They all have the same young girl in them. She looks maybe twelve or so, and the resemblance between her and Harris is striking.

"Is this your daughter?" I ask.

"What?" He pops his head out of the kitchen and sees what's in my hand. "No, that's my sister."

Of course, that makes sense. "Does she live around here?"

A peculiar look of sadness transforms his expression, and I'm sorry I said anything because I really enjoyed his humming.

"She died when she was fourteen."

"Oh, no. I'm sorry...I didn't...." It's one of those awkward conversations I never learned how to handle. I add *socially inept* to my list of faults.

"No need to apologize. I keep her picture out because it helps me remember."

I nod. Of course he'd want to remember his sister, but it sounded like there was more to it than just that. "What do the pictures help you remember?"

"Who I am."

And who are you, Caden Harris? I want to say. The more I get to know, the more I see he has so many layers to him. Seeing him in his house, humming and making dinner, there's no way I can also see him as Mike's main henchman. The two aren't compatible.

And yet, he's worked for Mike for over two years.

"Why would you forget?" I ask.

It's not the question he's expecting. I get the impression he wants to tell me something badly, but instead he shakes his head and smiles. "No time for twenty questions if you want to eat tonight. Pasta's not going to cook itself."

He goes back into the kitchen, but I can't help but notice he's not humming anymore.

⁂

My first few days with Harris are easy. We don't discuss his sister or my past anymore. Instead, our conversations are light. It's altogether unsettling how quickly I forget who he is when I'm in his presence. I'm sure he must be keeping in contact with Mike somehow, but he never does so in front of me.

A few days after my arrival, he sheepishly hands me new clothes, assuring me they aren't the ones from the trunk. I thank him and carry them to my room. I hang them up carefully, stopping only when I get to the green sundress I never went back to pick up. I decide to wear that one first, and I put it on before heading downstairs.

Harris is working on his laptop in the living room, but he looks up and gives a nod of satisfaction when I enter. "Green does look good on you."

"How did you know?"

"I had to keep an eye on you."

I put my hands on my hips. "So you could report back to Mike?"

He stops typing completely and looks up, holding my attention for several long seconds before answering. "To keep you safe."

It's the same thing he always says, and I wonder how many times I'll have to hear it before I believe it. Is there even a number that high?

He's so easy to believe here in his house, but all I have to do is picture him next to Mike and all my trust in him disappears.

"I want to," I tell him. "I want so badly to believe you."

"I know."

From anyone else, it would have sounded conceited, but it doesn't when he says it.

"I know because I want as well," he says.

"What do you want?"

He shakes his head. "I have to get back to work. Did the rest of the clothes fit?"

"I only tried this one on, but I'm sure the others will." I swallow. "Thank you."

His focus is already back on his laptop. "You're welcome."

It's not much later when he comes looking for me. I'm in the kitchen, looking through his cabinets, trying to find something to fix for lunch.

"Athena."

There's a catch in his voice, and I suspect I'm not going to like what he has to say. My knees wobble, but I force myself to be calm. He'd told me he'd keep me safe, and I'd told him I'd trust him. This is a test. I have to believe in something, it might as well be him.

"Yes." My voice doesn't convey the fear I feel.

"It's happening sooner than I anticipated. Mike wants to have a video conference tomorrow."

We hadn't even discussed what those would encompass, but just the words *Mike* and *video conference* have me feeling like I've been punched in the gut.

"What exactly will I have to do?" I ask.

He sighs and sinks into a nearby chair at the kitchen table. "It's up to me, basically. But I know he'll want to ensure you're in some sort of subservient role. That you're obeying. That I handle it when you don't."

I grit my teeth. "And you can do that in a video chat?"

"*We* can do that in a video chat."

"I'm a good actress."

"Good will sign your death certificate. You have to be fucking brilliant."

Chapter Seventeen

I'm being brilliant. I'm being brilliant. I'm being brilliant.

Or at least that's what I'm telling myself the next day as I stand in front of the bathroom mirror in nothing but skimpy lingerie. Harris has been in a foul mood all day and if I didn't know better, I'd say he's dreading this as much I did. We've gone over and over our plan for the call, and each time we run through it, he grows more and more distant.

I slip a sheer nightgown over my head, and I'm ready. Harris waits for me in the living room. He's still frowning. He hasn't smiled all day and not even attempted to hum.

The computer is set up beside him, but something's out of place. That's when I notice the pictures of his sister are gone. I wonder why, but I'm not about to bring it up. If talking about his sister a few nights ago killed his good mood, I don't even want to know what talking about her today will do.

Besides, there isn't time.

"You need to get into position," he says, and somehow with just those six words, all traces of the man I've observed over the last day disappear. What is most surprising, though, is my reaction.

Almost instantaneously, I find myself slipping into the role I played for so many years. The role I donned almost without thought. It feels wrong now, like a shoe that's too small or perhaps one that almost fits, but rubs the skin in such a way you know there will be blisters left behind. I will not get out of this call unmarked.

I bend my knees in order to kneel beside Harris and happen to glance his way. His eyes are shut in what looks like pain. He will not get out unmarked either.

"Two minutes," he says, and I nod, unable to speak.

I jump when his hand lightly strokes the back of my neck.

"I wish there was another way," he whispers.

That's all he has time to say, and he clears his throat right as the call comes in.

I don't plan to look at the computer at all. Harris agreed with me yesterday that there shouldn't be a need. I'm afraid to look at Mike. I'm afraid if I do, everything I feel and think will be reflected in my eyes and it will not do anyone any good for Mike to see the amount of hate within me.

"Harris."

My stomach threatens to heave at the sound of his voice. Harris moves his foot ever so slightly toward me to where it grazes my knee. I slide my hand to brush the top of his shoe and somehow it's enough. I know I can get through this.

"Sir," Harris replies.

"I don't have long. Give me an update."

I don't have long might be the best words ever to be spoken, and I give silent thanks that perhaps this won't be as bad as I feared.

"It's going the way we thought it would. She's a bit taciturn and hesitant, but with the proper incentive, she performs better."

Performs. It's a little hint that what we're doing is an act. That he is still who I glimpsed yesterday and soon this will be over. I just had to play my part.

Be fucking brilliant.

"Where is she now?"

"Kneeling here beside me."

"Let me see."

Be fucking brilliant.

"Stand up, slut," Harris says.

I stand to my feet, keeping my head down.

"Why does she have so many clothes on?" Mike asks.

"So you can watch her do this." Harris is adjusting the camera to give Mike an eyeful. "Strip."

I've never been naked in front of Harris. When we practiced, he didn't have me undress completely. I now see that was a mistake. I'm clumsy and uncoordinated.

"Excellent work, Harris. I can see her tremble from here."

"Thank you, sir. She didn't do it quickly enough the first time. I had to punish her."

"How?"

"She didn't eat last night."

"Hmm, that's well and good, but I found with her, something corporal works best."

"Thank you for the advice. I'll use that next time."

I've removed the nightgown, and now I'm fumbling with the bra. I don't want to be naked in front of Harris and I'm not sure why it bothers me so much.

"Faster," Harris says in a rough voice. "You have two seconds to get completely nude. As it is now, you don't get clothes for the next 48 hours."

"That's cruel, Harris," Mike says, but he's laughing.

"No need for them anyway. It'll save time when I want to fuck."

I'm naked now, but still not looking at either man. *Be fucking brilliant.*

I'm trying.

"Now that is always a sight to behold," Mike says. "She has a body made to take dick."

"That she does. I'm so hard, I could bust something wide open." There's the sound of unzipping and I freeze. Harris is taking his pants off. This isn't part of the script.

"I'll start with her ass. Bend over the arm of the couch, slut."

I'm really trembling now. *What the hell is he doing?* and *Please don't fuck me in front of Mike,* battle each other in my mind, but I do what I'm told and position myself over the couch.

"I think I'll take her ass dry as punishment for being slow," Harris says. "Is that corporal enough?"

"That'll definitely take care of your need to bust something wide open."

"True, and she won't be slow again."

"She won't be sitting down, either."

Harris moves into position behind me, and I'm about to throw up, yell, pass out, or maybe do all three when his foot nudges mines. It doesn't bring me the same level of comfort as it did earlier.

"I'd like to stay and watch," Mike says. "If for no other reason then to hear her scream. But I do have to go, so maybe next time."

"Sounds good. Talk later."

"Make it hurt," Mike commands, and then he clicks off.

I hold my breath, half expecting Harris to push his way into me.

There's a few seconds of silence, and then Harris grumbles, "Mother fucking hell," and drops a blanket around me. I exhale in pent-up relief, but I'm still shaking as I pull the blanket tightly around me and sit on the couch.

Harris stomps into the kitchen and takes a bottle of what looks like scotch and pours a good amount. He takes two sips and then throws the glass against a far wall.

He bends over with his hands on his knees. "I'm too damn old for this shit."

I watch in total silence, not wanting to disturb him, or maybe I'm afraid to. It's yet another side of Harris, and I wonder how many there are and if I'll ever feel completely comfortable around him.

He finally stands up and gathers two bottles of water from the refrigerator before coming back to the living room and sitting down next to me.

"I'm sorry." He passes me a water. "I didn't plan on changing what we'd planned, but he wasn't buying it. I had to."

"S'okay," I say, still waiting for the shaking to stop.

"It's not. There's nothing about any of it that's okay." He runs a hand through his hair. "And I don't have damn clue what to do the next time he wants to call."

I press my lips together. I had plenty of clues. Unfortunately, none of them were remotely appealing. I try to open my water bottle, but I can't seem to get my fingers to work.

"Are you okay?" He takes the bottle and opens it for me.

I bring the bottle to my lips as I nod and somehow manage to pour it all over my lap.

"You're shaking like crazy. Are you cold?"

"No." I shake my head. "I don't know what's wrong with me."

"I scared you, didn't I?"

"A bit," I admit.

"Scared myself, too."

I wisely decide not to ask him what that means.

I wake up that night around three in the morning. My sleep schedule is all screwed up, and knowing I won't be able to go back to sleep anytime soon, I tiptoe down the stairs and head outside. I sit in one of the chairs I sat in days earlier when I first arrived at Harris's house.

He was quiet all throughout dinner, only speaking when I asked him a direct question. After we finished eating, I shoved him out of the kitchen, promising to clean up everything myself. He stayed away from me for the rest of the evening and I didn't see him before I went to bed.

The door behind me opens and he steps out.

"Been out here long?" he asks.

"Just a few minutes."

"I didn't mean to scare you this afternoon," he says.

"I know."

"And yet I did." He steps forward so he's in front of me, but not facing me. "And I'll probably have to do it again."

"I know."

"Do you, Athena?"

I stand up and move behind him. Something tells me to touch his shoulder, but I hesitate. This type of touch is like a foreign language to me. I know all about bringing a man pleasure, but next to nothing about how to bring him comfort.

Never going to learn if you don't practice.

I place my hand on top of his shoulder. He sucks in a breath, and I wonder if he knows how difficult that simple move was for me.

"I gave you my word that I'd trust you," I say. "You haven't let me down yet."

"Give me time."

"You could have ratted me out to Mike anytime you wanted and you didn't. Not just today, but lots of other times, too. Well," I said remembering, "except for that first night with Theo."

"What first night with Theo?"

"When you told Mike I was late."

He turns around to face me. "I didn't tell Mike you were late."

"You didn't?"

He shakes his head.

"Then who did?"

"I don't know. It might have been Theo. I promise it wasn't me."

I tilt my head. The moonlight makes his hair look lighter then it really is, and his eyes are more intense than they've ever been before.

"Why are you so nice to me?" I ask.

"What?"

"Why are you so nice to me?" I repeat.

His voice drops an octave. "I thought that much was clear." He cups my face and runs his thumb over my bottom lip. "I want all good things for you. I want you to be safe, doing a job you're excited about. I want you to never feel like you have to look over your shoulder for fear of who you'll find there. I want too damn much, Athena, and I'm the worst kind of hypocrite there is because when you stood naked in my living room, I just wanted you period."

I gasp, and he gives me a sad smile.

He's been beating himself up over this all day. Because a naked woman stood before him and he wanted her. I could go back to bed and pretend like I never heard him. I'm pretty sure that's what he wants, and he'll act like we never had this conversation in the morning.

Or....

I cover his hand with mine. "Caden."

"Don't, Athena."

"Don't you dare tell me what to do, Harris. I'm damn tired of people telling me what to do."

And with that, I pull him to me and brush my lips against his.

He's frozen in place. Either that or he's told himself he's not going to respond. I pull away slightly and whisper, "Damn it. Kiss me back." But again, he doesn't move. "Please," I add.

Just when I think he's going to stay in that same spot forever, he groans and takes me in his arms. His head tilts, and his lips cover mine, and *holy hell* I had no idea.

This. *This* is a kiss. This urging of his mouth in time with mine. The way he tastes and takes and gives and licks. I didn't know so much could be conveyed in a kiss and I almost weep that it's taken me so long to understand. What had been missing with Isaiah, was present with Harris. I don't know if it's because Isaiah was somewhat familiar or if Harris still has that hint of danger.

His hands come up to frame my face and he deepens the kiss.

Never. It's never been like this with anyone. And I want more and I don't want it to stop. He takes a step closer and it's obvious that he wants more and doesn't want it to stop, either. He runs one of his hands down my side, ghosting my breast, and my body shivers in a new and decadent way. I shouldn't be feeling like this. Isaiah is a good man, I should be drawn to him, but I'm not. It's Harris who's touch is awakening those parts and feelings I long thought dead.

I need to touch more of him, and I slide my hand down his back, enjoying the hardness of his muscles beneath my fingertips. I can tell he is beautiful beneath his clothes, and I almost laugh because whoever heard of a man being beautiful?

I'm desperate to see him. My fingers dip under the hem of his shirt and inch it upward. His skin is hot to my touch. Hot and hard and lean and I've never *wanted* so much before.

But he pulls back. "I can't." He's panting, his forehead presses against mine. "I can't, Athena."

"Why?" Why when I'm so close and need so much is he shutting the door to keep me where I am? Hot tears burn in my eyes. He knows I'm no good. Why would he want me?

"Don't. Don't cry." He sweeps his thumb beneath my lashes, catching my tears before they fall. "And don't think for a minute that I don't want you so bad I'm nearly blind over it."

"Then why?"

"Because when we make love, it's going to be when we're both free."

"But —" I want to protest, but he stops me with a finger over my lips.

"No buts. I will have you, count on it, but not like this. Not when you're here this way and not when you have no choice about where you live."

Even with his words, the doubt that consumes me is painful. "Are you sure?"

And then he completely steals my heart, "I'm more than sure. When I finally have you in my bed, I'm going to do more than just steal a kiss." His mouth drops to my ear and his words are wicked and hot in my ear. "I'm going to *feast* on you. I'm going to fucking *devour* you."

Chapter Eighteen

We're having dinner two nights later when Caden gets a phone call. He's not happy; he's frowning when he sees the display, frowning when he takes the call to the other room, and frowning when he returns.

"I have to go," he says. "I hate leaving you."

I hate it, too. I don't want to be alone in this house. "Is it him?"

He nods, and even though I don't like it, maybe it's better for him to go now. Maybe that means we won't have to have a another web session anytime soon.

"Go on," I say. "I'll be fine."

But he doesn't look convinced.

I'm cleaning up the kitchen shortly after Caden leaves when I hear a knock on the back door. I ignore it at first. Who knocks on the back door? Besides, it's the first time Harris has left me in the house alone, and I'd be lying if I said I wasn't just a little freaked out that the minute he's gone someone's knocking on the door.

But whoever it is, they're dedicated to getting my attention and I decide I can at least peek out the window to see who it is. I head up the stairs to look at them from the second story. That way, they won't see me checking them out.

Once upstairs, I pull the curtain aside and look down.

Isaiah?

What is he doing here? My heart leaps into my chest at the sight of him. But then I remember Harris told me Isaiah was married, and all I feel is conflicted. I want to believe Harris hasn't lied to me about anything.

In the end, it comes down to one of two things: Isaiah is married, or potentially everything Harris has told me over the last few days has been a lie. I don't know which would hurt more.

I scurry down the stairs. At least I can talk to Isaiah. See what this visit is about.

I crack the door open a bit, and I'm confronted with Isaiah's troubled brown eyes.

"Isaiah?" I ask. "What are you doing here? Come in."

"No, I can't. It's not safe. I'm only here now because Harris left. It's dangerous for me to be in there." He glances around the yard. "You, too."

"Harris dangerous?" I can't even fathom it anymore. "Nah, I'm safer here than I've been anywhere."

He looks hurt. "Safer than you were with me?"

"Mike trusts him."

"Yeah, that's what I want to talk with you about. Will you come out?"

I look back inside. I don't know how long Harris will be gone. But it wouldn't hurt to just step outside. Besides, it's Isaiah.

"Okay," I say. "But only for a second. Give me a minute."

I finish tidying up the kitchen, and by the time I make it outside, he's pacing around the yard.

"What's up?"

He stops and runs his fingers through his hair. "Mike knows you were with me. He's going to ruin me. He's started a rumor I'm married. I should...I should have listened to you."

My stomach plummets. There's only one way Mike would know. Only one person who would have started that particular rumor. I close my eyes. I won't cry over Harris. I won't. At least not now.

One day I'll let myself cry for the man I thought he was. And bitter, bitter tears for what I thought we could be together. I try not to think about being in his arms, how good and protective they felt around me. I don't want to recall the way he set my body burning with his words alone.

Because if I do, I'll have to accept that I mean nothing to him and that hurts too much.

I must be showing more emotion than I thought, because Isaiah's looking at me with pity. "I'm sorry. I know it's hard to take in. I wish...I wish he really was everything you thought he was. That he could be for you what I'm not."

"I"m that easy to read?" I sniffle.

"I'm sorry, but yeah, your face gave it away."

"It's okay. You'd think I'd be used to it by now. Being disappointed in people."

"Have I disappointed you?"

It's a bittersweet truth, but the truth all the same. "No. No you haven't."

"Let's get out of here." His eyes are wide with excitement. "Let's go tonight. I can take you away from all this. Let me, Athena."

It's so tempting. To leave Vegas once and for all. I glance over my shoulder to the house behind me. It's what I told Harris I wanted, wasn't it? To leave his house.

"I can't be him. I know. But please." He touches my shoulder. "I would cherish you. Always."

I'm a fool and a half because standing before me is a fine, upstanding man and my heart is breaking because of Mike's henchman. I should be jumping and down that Isaiah wants to run away with me. And, the truth is, had he bought it up before my hospital stay, I would have.

Being with Harris changed me. And even if it all turned out to be a lie on his part, the feelings I felt were real, and I know now what it means to really *feel.* Will I ever have that with Isaiah? I sigh because even if the answer is 'no,' I'll at least be safe.

I smile at him. "Should I pack?"

Something a lot like victory surges in his eyes. "No, leave it all here. You don't want those clothes. Paid for with Mike's dirty money." My protest is on the tip of my tongue, but it dies there because Mike pays Harris. Everything Harris buys is bought with dirty money.

"Let's get out of here," I say, and we head toward his car.

We haven't been in the car long when I get the feeling something's not right. I can't put my finger on it. It's not Isaiah. His focus is solely on the road. Maybe it's me. I'm finally on my way out of the mess that has been my life for the latest ten years and I'm not experiencing the joy I thought I would.

Caden's words echo in my head.

"I want all good things for you. I want you to be safe, doing a job you're excited about. I want you to never feel like you have to look over your shoulder for fear of who you'll find there."

I blame Caden. It's his fault I want to do more than just survive. I want to delight in life as well. I want to feel the way I felt when he pulled me to his chest and whispered his plans for me in bed.

"Not like this. Not when you're here this way and not when you have no choice about where you live."

I'd thought his words sweet when he first said them, but sitting in Isaiah's car, I'm reminded of another night, not too long ago.

"Shhh. Let me do this. You can tell me to stop at any time and I will." Isaiah pressing me down on the couch. "Are you okay with this?"

Two different men. Two different responses to me. One who wanted to give and one who wanted to take.

A shiver runs down my spine.

I turn my head slightly so I can watch Isaiah. He looks rather calm for a man who supposedly has Mike out to ruin him. In fact, he looks nothing like the nervous man who knocked on Harris's door.

I glance out the window, and we're not on a highway, but in a residential part of town. An upper-class neighborhood. Something's way off. I rest my fingers on the door handle.

"Where are we?" I'm trying to sound natural and not like I'm suddenly scared as hell about what's going on.

"I need to drop something off before we head out of town." He doesn't shift his gaze from the road.

"Here?" Why would Isaiah be in this part of the city?

"Around here. Not much further."

I tell myself this is Isaiah. I've known him since elementary school. He won't hurt me. He's a pastor. I try to calm myself by reasoning that I'm highly emotional after the last few weeks and it's perfectly normal to second guess everyone's motives.

Nothing's working.

My hands are trembling when we pull onto a driveway that is secluded and set off the road. I can't even see the house until we continue along the winding drive. It's huge. A brick fortress that looks inhospitable and cold.

"You know the people who live here?" I ask, as he pulls to a stop in front of the garage.

"You could say that." He presses a button on the car's visor and the long garage door starts to open. "I live here alone. I'm a recent widower."

I'm staring in horror at the car that ran me off the road.

Chapter Nineteen

I have my seat belt off and the car door open in under two seconds. Within four seconds, I'm running down his driveway. I don't stop to think about where I'm going. I'm just running. I had the element of surprise; I don't think he anticipated me taking off like I did, but he's got me beat with strength and speed.

He's behind me, and he's gaining ground. I push myself to run faster, but I'm too weak, and it's too dark, and I don't know where I'm going. I look over my shoulder to see how close he is, and that's a mistake, because I trip over a twig and land on my knees.

He's on top of me almost immediately and pins me to the ground. "Stop it."

"It was you!" I'm jerking as hard as I can, but I can't get away. "You're the one in the car. You killed that woman. Oh my God, she *was* your wife. You killed your wife."

His eyes are wild and dangerous. "Yes, she outlived her usefulness. Something you're getting pretty close to doing yourself."

"You're a sick fuck."

"And you're a dumb whore. It's pathetic how easily I had you eating out of my hand. I bet you'd have believed anything I told you." He brings my arms over my head and ties them together. "But that little outburst did confirm what we suspected. Harris told you I was married, didn't he?"

Harris!

He hadn't been lying after all.

Isaiah's the one who has been telling lies. And I believed every fucking one.

"What I don't understand is why you spread your legs so easily for him and acted like an ice queen around me."

I try to kick him, but I can't move my legs with the way he's on top of them.

"What's wrong? Your old childhood friend not good enough for you? You think your whore cunt is something special? Just give me a few days; I'll show you how not special it is."

I spit in his eye.

I barely register the fist headed my way before it collides and I slip into darkness.

I wake up with a jerk. The light in the room I'm in is too bright and it's hurting my head. The white walls intensify the light. I squint and look around. I'm on a bed and I'm naked. There are two windows, but they're covered from the outside. I'm assuming I'm still in Isaiah's house.

I swing my legs over the bed and I'm shocked at how weak I am. How long have I been out of it? There's a glass of water by the bed, but I'm afraid it's drugged, and I won't let myself drink it.

Isaiah.

His name resonates in my head. I can't believe any of this. How did he manage to completely snow me? Has he been working with Mike this entire time?

My blood runs cold at that thought, because if Isaiah works for Mike, they're probably aware of what Harris has been doing to protect me. If only I had a way to warn him.

Starting on the *if onlys* is a bad idea, because now I go through them all.

If only I'd trusted Harris sooner.

If only I hadn't opened the door to Isaiah.

If only I hadn't been so stupid.

I go to the door and turn the knob. It's locked, of course. Just that little bit of walking has zapped all my energy, and I slowly make it back to the bed. How long has it been since I ate?

It's too hard to think. Isaiah must have given me something for my mind to be this fuzzy.

I lay back on the bed, and my eyes close.

Closing my eyes is a bad idea, because that's when the voices come and I see flashbacks of the faces of my past.

My dad's grief before he ran off.

A knowing smile.

"I don't even know your name."

"Mike. Mike Randolph."

"I'm a pastor."

The bluest eyes I've ever seen.

"Goddess of wisdom?"

"I need you to trust me."

The last breath of a woman who paid for her mistakes with her life.

"Not the police."

The frightened whisper of a young girl who had no idea the evil that waited for her.

"Thank you."

They surround me in my sleep, whispering of last chances and missed opportunities. They tell me it's too late now and I'm never going to get out. I'm pressed into the bed and I feel the weight of the last ten years struggle to keep me there. It's not really a fair fight with all of them against me.

"Wake up." Someone slaps my face.

I think the suffocating memories of the past are preferable to the person beside the bed, and I try to sink back into sleep.

"Wake up."

I crack one eye open when Isaiah slaps me again. "Go to hell."

He laughs. "No doubt, but I have a feeling you'll get there first."

He's binding me to the bed. I struggle, but I'm still weak, and he stops my protest with little effort.

"What the fuck did you drug me with?" I ask.

"Just a little something."

It occurs to me I should keep him talking and if there's one thing I know, it's that men love talking about themselves. I bet he's no different.

"Are you really a pastor?" I ask.

"Wouldn't you like to know? People think I am, that's the important part."

"But Mike knows?"

"Mike knows everything, why do you think I suddenly popped up in your life? He knew all about the soft spot Harris has for you." A knowing grin covers his face. "Or had for you. Who do you think called him tonight and what do you think Mike did once your boyfriend showed up?"

It's too horrible to think about. Harris can't be dead. He can't be. I brace myself against the rage and grief building within me, because I know if I give into it, I will succumb to hysterics. I take a deep breath. "Harris killed him."

His laugh is cruel. "Unfortunately not. Mike sent me a text right before I came in here." He grabs my chin, forcing me to look at him and brings a knife up to my face. "No more questions. Keep talking, and I'll cut your tongue out. Mike was way too lenient with you. Let you get away with too much."

My entire body goes rigid at the sight of the knife because I have no doubt he'll use it.

"There we go," he says, obviously pleased with the fear in my eyes. "Since you're nice and quiet, I'll tell you what's going to happen. I have three buyers coming in a few hours and before they buy, they want a taste. That's why I have you tied up. Have you ever had three men before? I bet you have. Filthy slut." He runs the knife down my torso and positions the tip at my inner thigh. "You will do anything they want."

I hear him talk through the fog in my brain. At the same time I'm going through the possible options to escape. I'm totally fucked if he keeps me tied up, but I'm not going to ask for anything with him holding the knife.

"Better get your rest now. You have a busy night tonight." He stands up, and I think he's leaving, but he turns back and sits down. "You better hope and pray one of them likes you enough to purchase you." He takes the knife and holds it to my throat. "One way or another, you won't be here tomorrow. Understand?"

I nod.

"Good." He puts the knife on the table beside the bed and starts to undo his pants. "I've changed my mind. I think it's only fair I take a trial run, don't you think? See firsthand what I'm selling."

I make up my mind. I'm not leaving this room alive. I'll be damned if I'm going to let someone buy me. I faced this decision ten years ago, and I don't have it in me for another ten. But that doesn't mean I'm going to go easy. I focus all my attention on my right hand. If I can get it undone, I'll have a fighting chance.

Isaiah's taken his pants off ,and I drop my eyes to his erection. "If it's all the same to you, I'll just go on back to sleep. I don't see anything here worth staying awake for."

"Bitch, I'll wipe that fucking smile off your face."

"Yes, but you'll still have a small dick." I wasn't sure what I was doing. If I could somehow get my hand on that knife....

But how, with my hands tied? I twist and wiggle my right hand. I think maybe the rope gives a little.

Above me, his eyes grow murderous. He grabs my face with one hand and holds the knife in the other. "What did I tell you about that mouth? Let's see how sassy you can be when I'm finished with it."

I grit my teeth. No way is he getting near my mouth with that knife. I'm just buying time, trying to wear him down, until I can get my hand free. I contort my wrist this way and that. Yes The rope is looser, I just need more time.

A loud crash comes from somewhere above us, and Isaiah freezes. "They're early. Shit." He puts the knife down on the table and straightens his pants.

Damn, the knife is further away. I'd worry about that next. For now, I needed to get my hand free. I pull as hard as I can, but the rope doesn't budge. *Fuck.* I've got to get at least one limb free before those men get here.

Someone's pounding on the door. "Open up! Police!"

My heart leaps to my chest, not because it's the police, but because I recognize the voice and *he's not dead.*

Unfortunately, Isaiah recognizes it as well and moves fast. When Harris busts through the door, gun raised, Isaiah's on the bed. And the knife is at my throat once more.

Chapter Twenty

Game's up, Martin. Drop it." Harris has the gun pointed at us both. "Besides, haven't you heard what happens when you bring a knife to a gun fight?"

Isaiah is frighteningly calm. "I'm not fighting, though. I'm simply going to cut your whore's throat if you don't turn around and leave."

"I can't do that."

"Then her blood is on your hands."

Harris is still standing with his gun drawn, and he can't do anything because I'm too close to Isaiah. I catch Harris's eyes and I try to silently tell him how sorry I am. For everything. The knife is pressing deeper into my skin, I feel a trickle of something that's probably blood.

I twist my right hand again and give it a tug. Isaiah thinks I'm struggling with him and doesn't look at my hands. I wiggle my left fingers to get Harris's attention. His eyes flicker to me and I hold up five fingers, then four. Isaiah's watching the knife. Three. Harris nods, understanding something was happening at one. Two. I take a deep breath. One.

I pull with all my strength and my right hand is free. I use the few seconds Isaiah is rendered shocked to push the knife away from me. Harris takes his cue and restrains Isaiah.

"Damn, bitch." Isaiah is spewing curses, but he's no longer a threat. Harris waves another officer inside the room to deal with him. Then, with a face void of expression, he turns to me.

Without talking, he drapes a blanket over me that someone has passed him, and begins to untie the rest of my limbs.

"How's your throat?" he asks.

I put a hand up to check and there's blood, but not much. "I'm good. It'll stop in a minute."

He presses a cloth to it.

"Harris, I wanted —"

His finger on my lips stops me from saying anything further. "Shh, not right now. Later. Let's get you somewhere safe where you can be checked out."

"I don't want to go back to the hospital."

"It's for your safety. We don't know what drug he gave you. If it all goes well, you won't have to stay overnight."

Where will I stay?

I don't ask the question out loud.

The hospital agrees I don't have to stay overnight. I'm sitting in my room, wearing secondhand clothes when Harris walks in.

"No scrubs this time?" He's leaning against the door frame, watching me.

I shake my head. "No, they had someone donate these for cases like me."

He sighs and pushes away from the door and stands near me. "Where are you going to stay?"

I bite my lip. "There's a women's shelter that's offered me a space."

"Is that what you want?"

I look up at him, and I feel so old. He told me I didn't have to worry about any charges being brought against me. To be honest, until he mentioned it, the possibility hadn't crossed my mind. "I don't know what I want."

He sighs and sits down next to me. "I've only ever wanted one thing."

"Did you get it?"

"Not yet."

"Mmm." I don't know what else to say.

"I wasn't allowed to tell you," he says.

"That you were a cop?" I look at him sideways. He has his badge attached to his shirt, and it's still throwing me for a loop that he's a cop when I see it.

"Right. I wanted to. But I'd been undercover for what? Almost three years? It was too risky and would have put the entire operation in jeopardy."

I'm obviously still working off the effects of the drug, because it doesn't register with me until that exact moment that he has been working undercover the entire time I've known him.

"Operation?" I ask.

"We've been trying to bring Mike down for a long time. This was the closest we've gotten."

Closest we've gotten. "You didn't get him?"

"Athena, look at me." It's the first time he's ever used that tone of voice with me. That no nonsense commanding tone. I should be put off by it, but I'm not.

When he's certain he has my attention, he continues. "I had a choice to make. I could get Mike or capture Isaiah and save you. The timing wouldn't allow for apprehending both men."

I'm stunned by the meaning behind the words. "You picked me?"

"Yes, I picked you and I'd do it all over again the same way, no questions, no hesitations."

"But all those years you worked and Mike had no idea. You sacrificed that for me?"

"I did and we got Isaiah, too. You'd be surprised how dirty he is."

I touched the bandage on my neck. "I doubt that."

"You're right. Sorry. Besides, it would be a shallow victory if you had been sold into the sex market and I never saw you again. There will be other chances to get Mike. There was only one for you."

"Thank you," I whisper.

"I'm afraid it's not all good news." He takes a deep breath. "Mike didn't leave alone."

I don't want him to say any more, because I have a sick feeling in my stomach about what he's going to say next.

"We believe he took Vicki with him."

Vicki. I'll never forget her fear that day she tried to warn me. Why hadn't I listened? She had her head in the sink. That alone should have told me she was seriously freaked out.

"She tried to tell me. I should have listened." I close my eyes as the tears come.

"Don't blame yourself. The situation was out of your control."

There's a knock on the door, and a nurse comes in. "Just have some paperwork, Ms. Hamilton. Then we'll get you out of here."

Harris waits to stand up until she hands me the papers and a pen and leaves. "If you want to go to the shelter, I know them. They'll get you on your feet, help you find a job, get you settled and keep you safe. They're good."

I nod. I'm suddenly overwhelmed.

"On the other hand..." He reaches into his pocket and pulls out an envelope. "I believe this is yours. We found it on Isaiah."

I take the envelope and peek inside. "Oh my, God."

It's my ten thousand dollars. I'm free. It's enough to set me up for a time if I budget wisely.

"You can move to Indiana and work at a bookstore now," he says softly. "My card's in there if you need anything. I put my personal number on it as well."

I clutch the envelope to my chest. *Free. Free. Free.*

"Thank you," I say through the tears in my eyes.

"I meant what I said that night, Athena. I want all good things for you."

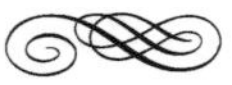

I decide not to make any hasty decisions, and I quickly find that not having had the ability to make my own decisions for so long has me second guessing everything. I don't really want to stay at a women's shelter. I'd like to get a hotel room, but for obvious reasons that seems weird.

I end up taking a cab to the far end of the Strip to a nice hotel I've never stepped foot in and where I'll just be Ms. Hamilton instead of a working girl. I am ridiculously tight with my money, counting and recounting every penny, working through my head over and over how long it can last and ways to make it last longer.

For two days, I stay in the room and do nothing. It's horribly decadent, but my body and mind need to recuperate. There are times I wake in a cold sweat certain there is a knife at my throat, and I know it will be some time before the nightmares become less frequent. After all, Mike is still out there somewhere.

During the day, I go from one extreme thought to another. My brain is finally processing that Harris was never in deep with Mike, never ratted me out, and was keeping me safe. Unlike Isaiah, who was playing me.

I take the card Harris left in the envelope and flip it over and over, not sure if I should call. Not sure what to say if I do call. Does he really care? Or was I just an assignment to keep safe?

In the end, there is one question I can't figure out, and it's that question that pushes me to call.

"Hello." He answers on the second ring and my knees threaten to buckle at the rough sound of his voice.

"Harris?"

"Athena? Is that you? Are you okay?"

I nod and then realize he can't see me. "Yes."

"Is there anything I can do for you? Do you need anything?"

"Just had a question for you."

There's relief in his voice when he answers. "Sure, what's on your mind?"

"That night I came to Theo's room and went to Mike's office the next day?"

"Yes."

"How did I make it back to my apartment?" I have been assuming it was Isaiah, but now, knowing what I do, I knew it couldn't be.

"I carried you. And left a note under Vicki's door so she would come see to you."

"Oh." As soon as I realized it couldn't be Isaiah, I'd frantically hoped it was him. It seemed too good to believe."

He takes a deep breath. "I had a meeting with him that morning. Apparently, Cybil tried to contact me to cancel it, but I never got her message. When I arrived, she told me to wait downstairs, that Mike was busy. I would have turned and left, but I heard..." His breath hitches. "I heard a wailing. I wasn't even sure it was human, coming from his office."

I'm straining to hear him because his voice is so low. "Cybil heard it too, because she jumped up right as I headed for the door. She tried to block me, and I told her if she didn't move out of my way, I'd shove the door up her ass."

I would have laughed at the thought of Cybil with a door up her ass had it been any other conversation I was having.

"I opened the door, and he was standing over you. With this look. Christ, I have nightmares about that look. I truly think he would have killed you if I hadn't arrived."

Harris takes a deep shuddering breath. "I didn't say anything. I picked you up and went down his private elevator to my car and drove you home. Then I called him and asked what the fuck he was doing. At that point, I didn't care if I blew my cover. To see you there....I couldn't...I thought of my...."

His sister.

Of course.

"Harris?" I ask. "How did your sister die?"

He's so silent I think the phone has gone dead, but then he speaks. "I don't want to talk about her over the phone. I don' t mind discussing it, but I want to do it in person. It's that important to me."

"Would you like to come here? I'm staying at a hotel."

"Only if you're okay with that. We can meet somewhere public if you'd like."

"No, I'm still not comfortable being outside a lot." I give him the name of the hotel and the room number. He agrees to come by later today.

He looks uncomfortable when he shows up hours later, and he hesitates before entering my room.

"Are you sure you're okay with this?" he asks.

"After everything you've done for me? I trust you completely." The man saved my life, for crying out loud. He kept me safe, and he's worried I don't trust him?

"How have you been?" He takes a seat on the couch in the room's small sitting area and I take a place beside him.

"Okay, I guess. I'm going to look for somewhere to live tomorrow. Talk to a job finder. Get some help finding a job."

The only thing holding me back is I have no idea what I want to do.

"Are you talking to anyone? Counseling? Therapy?"

"No." To be honest, I have't given anything like that a moment's thought.

He pulls a card from his pocket. "I have a few names and numbers here. I can vouch for them, and there won't be a charge."

I nod and take the card, but I have no intention of calling anyone. "Have you found Mike?"

"No, and he's resourceful. He could pop up anywhere. We'll bide our time and be patient, he'll show."

"And Vicki?" Biding time was fine for Mike, but Vicki was in danger.

The expression on his face tells me everything I need to know. "I'm sorry, Athena. There's nothing we can do until he surfaces."

I start to argue, but he stops me. "Don't. Don't think we haven't done everything we know to do in order to find her. Sometimes, the bad guys win the battle. All we can do is focus on the war."

He says the words, but they aren't easy for him to speak. "Is that how you deal with it?" I ask.

"It's the only way I'm able to deal with it. If I view it as a war, then I feel like I'm actively doing something. Even if that something is standing on alert."

"Is that what you told yourself about your sister?"

"Yes."

He stands up and begins to pace. He's made two turns of the room before he speaks again. "My mother was fifteen when she got pregnant with us. Her parents weren't prepared for her to have twins, and she was too young to have children, so we were placed in foster care. We were normal kids, I see that now, but we got shuffled around a lot. When we were thirteen, my sister said she'd found us a forever home. It was a man she'd met in the library."

I close my eyes. I could picture it all too easily. The young girl, desperate for a family and a place to fit in. A predator who just found his next victim.

"I begged her to let me meet him, but she kept putting it off. Saying it wasn't time. Then one day...she didn't come home." He sits down next to me, but he won't meet my eyes. "I was so angry with her. I thought she'd left me for him, and I was furious she didn't take me with her. I didn't understand why she wouldn't write or call or let me know where she was. Eighteen months later, she was dead. She had a tattoo on her that marked her as the property of a sex trafficker in New York City."

I think about the tattoo on my left hip that Mike had put on me years ago. It's been part of me for so long, I don't think of it most days. But now that I am thinking about, I want it off. Immediately. Yesterday. Five years ago.

"That's when I decided I was going to be a cop and stop the guys who prey on young girls."

"And you did it."

"There are days I hate my job. I hate acting like I'm one of them." He opens and closes his fist. "I always felt so dirty after I got home for the day. And discouraged because I knew I could never save all of them."

I don't think he's shared this part of himself with many people, and I'm honored he felt comfortable enough with me to do so. "Your sister would be proud."

He looks at me at those words, and I see traces of the lonely and lost boy he once was. "I watched you that day in the food court."

I wrinkle my eyebrows. "When I stalked Isaiah's wife?"

"The young girl you talked to."

"Probably didn't do any good."

"You don't know that. If someone had talked to you when you were sixteen, would you maybe have made different choices?"

"I'd like to think so."

"Then you did everything you could."

I'm suddenly hit with what he must feel everyday. "It never feels like it's enough, though, does it?"

"No," he says. "That's why we have to focus on what we know we can change and to try not to dwell on what we can't. And what you need to focus on is starting fresh. Are you leaving Nevada?"

"I don't know. I thought about going back to the South, but part of me wants to stay here. Maybe not Vegas, but the Southwest." It can be downright terrifying to have to make decisions. When I thought about where I wanted to live and knew I could go anywhere, I almost felt like burying my head in the sand. "Maybe I'll become a hermit."

"Never do that. You have too much going for you."

I remember his words from when I was at his house and wonder if he really meant them. He's not touching me at all today. In fact, it's like he's making a concentrated effort not to touch me. I want to say it feels like the only thing I have going for me is the ability to trust the wrong men. But I'm not ready to go there with him, so I'm quiet and hope there will be another day — some other time — for us to talk.

Chapter Twenty One

Five Months Later

It doesn't happen overnight, but I'm slowly learning who I am and how I fit into my new normal. Though I hadn't planned on going to a therapist, one day not long after Harris came by, I found myself in line to purchase whiskey at one in the morning. Unable to sleep because of thoughts of Mike, and haunted by thoughts of Vicki, I came to the conclusion I could sort everything out if I just had a drink. Or maybe enough to numb my brain so I didn't feel anymore.

Before I made it to the front of the line, I clued into what I was doing, and I left the store without the bottle. The next morning, I called the first therapist on the list Harris gave me. He was right about her, of course; she'd worked with women in my position before, and with her help, I started on my way to rediscover myself.

Within a few weeks, I started work at a local pet store and rented a small apartment on the other side of town from where I lived before. But I still jumped at loud noises, and sleep continued to be an issue.

Harris keeps in contact, but it's not like it was when we were at his house. I tell myself that those were stressful days for both of us, and our emotions were running high. That it was to be expected, shoved together the way we were.

And yet, my stomach still does flip-flops whenever he comes to the pet store.

About five months into my new start, he comes into the store unexpectedly on a Thursday. I've learned his routine, and he rarely deviates from it. Saturdays are when he buys cat food for Munchkin. He buys cans, which is funny because I remember a bag of dry food when I stayed with him.

"Hey," I say to him, and then raise my eyebrow because not only is it Thursday, he's not stopping by the cat food aisle. For a minute, I think he's heard about Mike or Vicki, but he's smiling and too relaxed to be bringing me such news. He reaches the counter.

"Can I help you with something?" I ask.

"I came to ask you a question," he says.

"Go for it."

"Will you go out to dinner with me tomorrow night?"

The leash I'm holding falls to the counter. "What?"

"Will you go out to dinner with me tomorrow night?"

"A date?"

"Yes," he answers.

I've done a lot of new things since I've been on my own, and I've had some new experiences, but I've done nothing resembling a date.

"Uh...I'm ... I should be.... I think...."

"Athena, it's just dinner. I promise."

I'm free the next night. I'm free most nights. And I've never been on a date.

"I'd really like to go on a date with you." My words come out in a rush, and I'm a bit embarrassed, but Harris doesn't act like he notices.

"I'll pick you up at your apartment at five?"

I'm going on a date.

My brain is still processing that information.

"Athena?"

"Yes. Five."

He smiles and says he'll see me then.

I'm a complete wreck the next day. Because I'm working the weekend, I have the day off. It really would have been better if I didn't have the day off. By noon, all my clothes are on top of my bed, and by two, I've vetoed every outfit I own. At three, I stand in front of my bathroom mirror and give myself a good talking to.

It doesn't work.

Nothing can erase the fact that I'm twenty-six and I've never been on a date. It doesn't matter that I've been with a lot of men. Not one of them stood before me and asked me to dinner. Not one of them wanted to spend the evening with me just because I'm me and not because I'd be naked at some point.

I walk back into my bedroom and shuffle through my clothes once more. It's another reason to hate Mike. The fact that I missed so much. For me, there had been no prom, no graduation, no first date. Nothing. But it's a conscious decision I make not to let that anger rule my life. To do so is to give him even more power over me, and I refuse to do that anymore.

When Harris rings the doorbell at five, I'm wearing jeans and a green silk top. It's not too casual and not too dressy. I open the door, and he's standing there, smiling and holding flowers.

Flowers.

"Hi," he says.

Flowers.

"These are for you." He holds them out. It's a combination of blue and white violets and they're the most beautiful flowers I've ever seen.

I tentatively take hold of them, supporting the glass vase they came in with one hand. "Thank you. I've... I've never gotten flowers before."

I can't stop looking at them.

"The white means 'take a chance on happiness,' and the blue means 'watchfulness.'"

"Appropriate," I say, catching his gaze and smiling. I step out of the way. "Would you like to come in while I put these down?"

"No, it's okay. I'll stay out here."

He's being respectful, and I appreciate that. However, I can't help but remember the way he kissed me and his promise after. My fingers remember the heat of his skin, and my body wants his hands on me again.

I place the flowers in the middle of my two-person kitchen table and hurry back outside. He's waiting with his hands in his pockets, and when he looks at me, there's a heat in his eyes I know I'm not making up.

"Ready?" He holds out a hand.

I nod and place my hand in his, and as our fingers entwine, I'm shaken once more because I can't remember the last time I simply held someone's hand. He squeezes his fingers briefly around mine as if he knows what I'm thinking.

"I made us reservations," he says.

We drive to a new restaurant not far from my apartment. It's an intimate bistro, and nothing like anything I went to when I was working for Mike.

In the last five months, I've gradually gotten over the fear that everyone who looks at me knows what I once did for a living. I remind myself I'm not the same person I was then and starting over means *starting over.*

Hardest to take are the looks men give me, though those are different now as well. Harris pulls out my chair when we're shown to our table, and I sit down with a sigh.

He raises an eyebrow as he takes his own seat. "Are you okay?"

I give him what I hope is a reassuring smile. "Yes, first date jitters."

"We've had a few meals together. This one just happens to be out in public."

"Not just first date with you. First date ever." I frown. "Well, if you don't count Mike, and I don't."

His eyes dim a bit at the mention of Mike, and I could slap myself for bringing his name up. I try to think of something — *anything* — to say to move the conversation in a different direction, but Harris beats me to it.

"Green is definitely your color. You look lovely tonight."

I feel my cheeks heat, and I dip my head. *Holy shit.* I just blushed. And I'm lovely. He thinks I'm lovely. I wouldn't have had the same reaction if he'd called me beautiful. Lots of men have called me beautiful, but he's the first to say I'm lovely.

"And the flush on your cheeks is charming," he says.

I look up. "Thank you."

The conversation could have gotten very uncomfortable after that, but he picks up the menu. "I have no idea what I want. What are you in the mood for?"

Living on my own and doing work I want to do has completely changed my outlook on things. I no longer fear sharing my opinion or speaking up about what I want. And as I've moved further and further away from the me of years past, I've learned I like the me I'm becoming.

I pick up my menu and scan it. "Know what I'd really like?"

"What?"

"A huge burger with lots of cheese and pickles and mayo. French fries. And any soda that's not diet."

He laughs, and I forgot how his laugh made my insides warm. "I think that might be last thing I expected you to eat."

"How about you? What's your favorite thing to eat?"

He looks back over the menu. "Club sandwich. Extra bacon, cooked to where it's almost burnt. Honey mustard to dip it in. French fries with pepper and a beer."

I wrinkle my nose at the mention of beer.

"You don't drink. I noticed that." He places the menu down and folds his hands on top.

"I did at one time, but then I didn't. I found that while the alcohol deadens the pain, it messes with your mind too much. Or at least it did mine."

"Why not a diet soda?"

"I don't like artificial sweeteners."

The waitress stops by to take our orders, and after she writes down my burger and his sandwich, she steps back. "You look familiar," she says to Harris.

Harris had been in the news shortly after rescuing me. He wasn't one to like being the center of attention, and he'd hated it.

"I just have one of those faces," he says.

"The papers said you were rescuing a woman from a trafficker," she replies, like he didn't say anything.

"I read that story, too." He glances at me. *To make sure I'm alright?*

"That poor woman. I hope she's doing okay."

"Me, too," he says and coughs.

The cough reminds her of where she's at and what she should be doing. "I'll go put this order in."

He leans back in his seat, exhaling deeply.

"You're a hero," I tease.

"Nah. Just doing my job."

"I think they're one and the same."

Our conversation over dinner is light and easy. Harris is easy to talk with and quick to joke and smile. It doesn't take long before I don't feel nervous at all. We finish eating, but we're still talking. He tells me about growing up in foster care, and I tell him stories from my childhood in the South.

He asks why I went to work at a pet store when I'd mentioned before I wanted to work in a bookstore, and in a soft voice, I share what happened with Mike and the books. And, I tell him that working around animals was a close second to owning one.

We arrive back at my apartment hours later, and my heart is racing as we walk up to my door. I'm not sure how to end the date. I don't want him to leave just yet.

I don't hesitate before saying, "Will you come inside?"

I can see he's conflicted about how to answer, and my heart plummets.

"I want to," he finally says. "But I think tonight's not the time."

I know my face shows my disappointment, but I feel a bit better when he's asks if he can take me to dinner tomorrow night.

"Really?" I ask, and at his nod I say, "Yes."

He leans his head toward mine, and my lips are hungry for his. I remember their taste and the way I felt when they touched mine. But all he does is lightly brush my cheek. I groan, and his lips tickle my cheek as he smiles.

"Believe me," he says in my ear. "I feel it too, but I want you to burn for me. To have you so needy that the merest hint of my touch sets you on fire."

"I'm there," I beg.

"Not yet. But soon."

The next evening, he brings a picnic and we eat outside at a nearby park. We sit on a bench for an hour afterwards watching people. It's strange and odd and wonderful and fun, this sitting around and talking. I tell him I want to one day be in a position to help other women escape the sex market. He tells me I'm well on my way.

I'm fairly certain he'll kiss me after the picnic date, but he once again only brushes my cheek. I run my hand down his arm and he just whispers, "Soon."

I decide to switch things up, so on Monday I call him and ask him if he would like to come to my place for dinner on Wednesday. I can tell I've caught him off guard, but he agrees.

It's when I'm bustling around Wednesday evening, twenty minutes before he shows up, trying to make everything perfect that I realize this might have been his plan the entire time. I have never invited a man to my apartment for anything. Sure, Mike came by, but he owned the place. And yes, I asked Harris over when I was in the hotel and he stopped by to pick me up, but it's not the same.

Was that why he hesitated? Does he know how big of a step this is for me and wants to make sure I'm ready? I wear something causal: jeans and a tank top. I'm not going to seduce him. He apparently has this whole thing well planned out and I'm going to let him lead.

But when he rings the doorbell and I let him in, there's something different about him. He's all heat and muscle, and the look in his eyes when he sees me is damn near flammable.

We sit down and eat the lasagna I prepared earlier in the day. Harris is charming as always, making me laugh at Munchkin's antics. He is somewhat reserved, though, like he's studying me. Watching for something.

"Thank you for inviting me over tonight," he says, when we're finished and the dishes are in the dishwasher.

"I wanted you to see me in my element. I saw you in yours."

"I'm not sure that completely counted, since we were trying to outsmart people the entire time."

I shake my head. "Those nights we'd go out in your backyard. That was the real you."

"Yes."

"I like the real you."

"The real me likes you, too."

"That night when we were out there, those things you said? You meant them?" I don't specify which things.

His eyes grow dark. "Yes, I meant every word."

"When you kissed me," I say, ready to talk about it that time in his backyard. "It was like nothing I ever felt before."

"For me, too." He takes a step closer to me.

I swallow. This is hard. This isn't me being paid or forced or in any way coerced. It's me as a woman and the woman I am is so very unsure about herself. "Will you kiss me again?"

"Now?"

I nod. "Please."

He takes two more steps, and then he's in front of me. Slowly, he lifts one hand to cup the side of my face, and I close my eyes when his thumb brushes my cheekbone.

Gently, so gently, I barely feel them, his lips sweep across my own in a soft kiss. I clutch his forearms. I want more.

"Please," I whisper, but he doesn't move. "Caden."

He takes a step back and brushes his thumb along the line of my lips. I part them and tease his fingertip with my tongue.

"I don't want you to do anything you're not comfortable with, or anything that doesn't feel good." His eyes are dark, and the longing in them takes my breath away. "I have to be honest: I'm scared as hell to do anything physical with you. I don't want to hurt you, and I want it to be good for you."

His honesty endears him to me even more "I'm scared, too. I keep thinking: what if I'm broken that way? What if I can't enjoy it?"

"Do you enjoy it when I kiss you?"

I decide to throw the gauntlet down. "I don't know; you only *really* kissed me that once."

His eyes flash with something, and he gives me a teasing smile before he frames my face with his hands. "Let's remedy that, why don't we?"

I only have time to nod before his mouth is over mine and *oh my God* yes, it is the same. I moan and pull him closer. It's an invitation he accepts, and his hands trail downward, pulling me tight against him.

His tongue teases my lips open, and I'm consumed and engulfed by all that is him and the only thing that doesn't feel good is the ache of needing more. I tuck my hand into the back of his waistband so my fingers rest right above his ass.

He pulls back. "Did that feel good?"

I want to whine that he stopped. "Yes. Very."

"Do you want to stop there or keep going?"

I make sure I'm looking him straight in the eye when I say, "I want to go further." And then to prove it, I take his hand and I lead him to my bedroom. I reach the middle of the room and turn to face him. "I've never in my entire life invited a man to my bedroom. You're the first."

He pulls me into his arms for another kiss. I'm beginning to think I could live on his kisses. Then he moves his lips to my neck, where he nips the skin, and I shiver.

"That good?" he asks.

"Very."

His hands slip down to my shirt. "Can I see you?"

I draw the shirt over my head, and I could bask in the appreciation in his look. I thought I'd feel awkward, like I did when I stripped in front of him while we were on the video call, but I don't. His look empowers me, makes me strong, and I want even more. "Your turn."

"I'm not near as gorgeous as you." But he pulls his shirt off anyway.

I suck in a breath at what is hidden under his clothes. There are round scars on his upper arms and one ragged line above his heart. "What happened to you? Who did this?" I ask in a small voice.

"Perils of living in foster care."

I point to one of the round scars. "Is that a cigarette burn?"

"It was."

"How could anyone do this to you?" I run a finger around the puckered skin on his arm.

"They were bigger than me."

"You're just like me, except you have scars on the outside and mine are all inside."

"Our pasts are what brought us both here tonight." He shakes his head. "Because of that, I can't find it in me to regret any of it."

I lower my head to his arm and kiss the scars there. "I knew you were beautiful beneath your clothes."

He chuckles. "Beautiful?"

I palm my hands over his chest and feel the strong beating of his heart. "Every inch of you is beautiful. Inside and out. I've never met anyone like you before."

He leans his head down and kisses me again, a bit more forcefully this time, and he walks me backward to the bed. I'm scared and excited and giddy and ready for more and wanting to stay in this moment forever. My knees hit the bed, and I sit down.

Harris drops to his knees and keeping his eyes on mine, unbuttons my jeans. I lift up so he can take them down, and when they're off, he pulls me to the edge of the bed, so I'm open and exposed to him. I still have my panties on, but I know he can see how wet I am for him.

He places kisses on my upper thigh while at the same time, teasing that sensitive area on on the back of my knee. His nips my skin closer and closer to where I ache for him.

"Are you burning for me yet?" he asks.

"Yes," I say, surprised I'm still able to form words.

"I'd like to make you come like this."

There have only been a few men who have attempted that, and I always ended up faking my pleasure. Of course, I'm an expert at faking. But I don't want to fake with Harris.

"You're tensing up," he says. "Is this okay?"

"Yes, I'm just..." I take a deep breath. "I don't want to be broken."

He places one last kiss on my kneecap, and then he joins me on the bed and pats a pillow. "Come up here."

I join him, aware as I do of the storm brewing in his eyes. It's a look of restrained longing and seeing it reignites my own. He props himself up on one elbow and his fingers circle my nipple.

"I'm going to explore every inch of you. We're both going to discover what turns you on." He runs his fingertip across my pebbled skin. "Because you are many, many things, but broken isn't one of them."

He starts slowly, touching and teasing me with light strokes everywhere. He's not in any hurry, and I feel my apprehension fade away, only to be replaced with a growing need. He explores my arms and my legs and other places I never thought of as sexy.

"Oh, yes," he says when he finds a spot that makes me thrash my head. "That spot makes you feel it deep inside doesn't it?"

It's only the crook of my elbow, but all he has to do is lick it and I almost come undone. "Yes."

"Wonder what would happen if I bit it?"

I can't even make a word when he does. I mumble something that makes no sense. He lifts his head and comes back up to kiss me and then settles into place at my side. I'm a quivering mess of desire and I'm going to explode when he touches me where I most want him to.

He drags one finger down my chest, across my belly, and I start to think *Please don't stop, please don't stop, please don't stop* because I think I know where he's going. The finger stops when it reaches my panties.

"I need you to take them off if you want me to continue," he says. "I think we've proven that you're not broken, and we don't have to go any further if you don't want to."

I take the panties off in less than three seconds.

He murmurs his approval and gets back into position by my side, his one hand still resting on my belly.

"I'm going to touch you more intimately now, are you okay with that?"

"Yes."

"I'm going to make you come with my fingers." His voice is rough. "Look at me while I pleasure you."

I open my eyes and meet his gaze right as his hand restarts its journey downward.

"I'm going to tease you until you're mad with lust, and then I'm going to dip my fingers deep inside you. Make you want me inside you so bad you don't think you'll be able to breathe without it."

"Yes, please. Now."

My hips lift off the bed when he circles that needy part of me, but I keep my eyes on his.

"Mmm, someone liked that," he says, doing it again.

Pretty soon, we start a rhythm. He teases my clit, and I jerk my hips, trying to get him inside me. I feel something building, and his gaze locks onto mine as he slowly sinks two fingers deep within me.

"Feel my fingers?" he asks. "My cock is bigger, and it's so goddamn hard."

Dirty talk has never really done anything for me before. It's always come across as crass. Men talking to get themselves more aroused. But when Harris speaks, looking me straight in the eyes, I feel his words. More than that, I want to feel him.

Then his thumb starts rubbing my clit while he thrust his fingers in and out, and all coherent thought leaves my head.

"Oh, God, Harris." My eyes close as an unfamiliar feeling builds.

"Open your eyes, Athena." His voice is thick with emotion. "I want to see your eyes when I make you come. I want you to see what your pleasure does to me."

I want to tell him he's talking crazy. How could my pleasure do anything to him? But I open my eyes, and I see I'm wrong. His expression is one of need and desire, surely, but I can tell it's more than what he's doing that makes him that way. It's watching me. My pleasure, my reactions are turning him on.

The building tide of my release is growing closer, and his fingers are good, but I want more. "Need you," I say.

"You have to come first," he says. "Trust me. It's killing me as much as it is you to wait. But you're going to come before I even think of getting inside you." He sinks his fingers in deeper. "You're so hot around my fingers. I can't wait to feel that heat around my dick. I'll probably go fucking insane."

He moves his fingers slightly, and it's so close. I feel it building and growing, and I'm desperate to reach it. His whispers encourage me, and my eyes nearly roll back into my head when the most incredible tempest of pleasure overtakes my body.

Something inside me shatters, and I'm not sure I'm even breathing as wave after wave crashes within my body. I'm muttering nonsense, and as my world tilts back to normal, Harris is kissing my cheek.

"I've never seen anything more perfect," he whispers.

"Oh my God." My body is still weak from this first orgasm, and I suddenly feel shy, which is the most absurd thing ever. I snort out a sob and a giggle at the same time.

He strokes my hair and captures my gaze. "Okay?"

"So much more than okay. I didn't know it could be like that."

Shock flickers across his expression, but I don't want to talk it about. I feel him hard and heavy against my thigh, and I want that feeling again, with him inside me this time. I reach down and stroke him.

"Now, Caden."

He waits only long enough to roll on a condom, and then he's between my legs and guiding himself to where I'm wet and needy. I bend my knees, giving him better access. My eyes close when I feel him brush his tip against me.

"Keep them open," he says. "I need your eyes on me."

Watching him as he enters me makes me feel more exposed than anything I've ever done, but I see the vulnerability in his expression, too, and I realize there are two of us. And we're together, and it's the most obvious thing, but I've never viewed sex as an act you do together. It's always been something done to me.

There's an ache of pure joy deep inside my soul when he's fully inside me, and he sees it and lowers his head so our foreheads touch.

"Athena," he whispers.

"You make me happy," I say, and I know it sounds silly, but they're the truest words I've ever spoken.

He raises himself so he's propped above me on one arm, and suddenly there aren't any words that fit the moment. He takes my hand with his free one and entwines our fingers. And he starts to move.

Oh.

My.

God.

It'd been incredible with his fingers, but now, like this....

Somehow, without even knowing, I'd locked a part of me away ten years ago. With his patience and honesty and gentleness, Harris had just taken the key and set it free.

Free. I squeeze his fingers and wrap my legs around his waist, anchoring myself to him as if the truth twists back into place and became crystal clear for the first time in ten years.

"Hold me," I whisper, fearing I'll take flight if he doesn't keep me grounded.

The wave is coming back, and it's even bigger, but that's okay because he's with me this time, and he's not leaving. His back arches above me. He's moving, and I'm moving with him, and it's the most natural and normal thing to do.

I grab hold of his waist with my free hand, loving the feel of his strength bringing me this pleasure. His hips speed up.

"With me this time," he pants. He takes our joined hands and slips them between us, teasing my clit. The simple movement makes the wave grow more, and my body tenses in anticipation. "Close?" he asks.

"Almost," I say, needing more but not wanting it to end.

His movements become slower, but more focused. Each stroke brings me nearer and nearer until I can't hold it back and I'm caught in that storm for the second time. He groans, and with one last deep thrust, his body shudders into mine.

My previous post-sex experience has left me unprepared for being in Harris's arms. I'm used to cleaning up and getting out of bed and, more often than not, facing the anger or shame of the person I've just been with. Then, when I was finally alone, facing my own anger and shame.

There is none of that with Harris. He excuses himself to dispose of the condom, but when I try to crawl out of bed, he pulls me back under the covers and slips his arms around me.

"You aren't leaving yet," he grumbles.

"I thought this would be the awkward part."

"There is no awkward between us," he says, and kisses my forehead. He takes my hand and kisses it.

"That was...." I shake my head, unable to find the words.

"I feel the same way," he assures me.

"I didn't know it would feel so good." I look up to see if he thinks I'm being silly, but he simply nods.

"It should always feel good," he says. "If I ever don't make you feel good, I'm doing it wrong."

"I've always had to fake before."

He lifts my chin with this finger. "No faking with me ever. If you're not into it, or if it doesn't feel good, let me know."

"Does that mean we're going to do it again?"

He chuckles. "Eventually, but not right this second. I'm not as young as I used to be."

Which is fine with me. I could stay here in his arms forever. We're silent for a few minutes, but then my hands get itchy to touch him, and I stroke his back and his chest. I trace one of his scars.

"Do they bother you?" he asks.

"No, not yours. Something of mine bothers me. I wish I could get rid of it," I say.

"You have a scar?"

I lift up on my knees and turn so my back is to him. "He marked me."

I don't have to tell him who *He* is. It's a black "M" right above my hip bone. I'm surprised he didn't see it that day when we performed for Mike on the webcam. But he was probably focused on other things at that time.

He runs a finger over it. "Bastard. I could kill him for that alone. Marking your skin."

"I'm lucky I was one of the older girls. He branded the new ones."

He nods. He would know, of course, working as closely as he did with him.

I look over my shoulder, trying not to be self-conscious that he's basically looking at my ass. His head tilts a bit, and he traces the *M* again.

"You know, the upper part of the M is rounded," he says.

"So?"

"I'm thinking, instead of getting it removed, why don't you have it made into something else? I think it could easily be turned into a butterfly."

I don't look at my ass a lot, but I remember the tattoo. I know exactly what it looks like. "A butterfly? I like that."

"And symbolic. Of you breaking away. Becoming something new. Being revived."

I turn around and pull him up so he's on his knees, too. "I had no idea you had a poet's soul, Caden Harris."

He laughs, but then I kiss him, and we fall back to the bed. And together, we both become something new.

EPILOGUE

One Month Later

I've almost decided it's ridiculous for me to have my own apartment. I spend all my free time at Harris's house. He insists, though, that it's important for me to have my own space and part of me sees his point, so I humor him.

Tonight is a big night. He's invited his boss and his wife over for dinner. It's the first time we'll entertain as a couple, our first double date. And I can't hide that I'm just a little nervous.

We talked about it last night as we sat in his backyard. I told him there was no need to bring his boss over. He adamantly stated he wasn't going to hide me, that I was part of his life and he wanted me to meet the other people in his life.

I didn't have a comeback for that.

I rush to his house after work. My clothes are already over there, and I want to take a quick shower before I start dinner. I'm humming as I turn onto his street. It's a habit I picked up from him, and it makes me happy.

My hum dies on my lips when I pull into his driveway. He's already home, and he shouldn't be for another hour. I try to tell myself it's nothing, but I can't shake the feeling that something's happened.

My suspicion is confirmed when I step inside. He's sitting on the couch, a worried look on his face, and though he tries to smile, it doesn't reach his eyes.

"What's wrong?" I ask.

"Come sit down with me."

"Oh, God. It's Vicki, isn't it?"

"Athena, come sit down."

I knew it. I knew she'd wind up dead. And it's my fault. If I hadn't been so wrapped up in myself that last day, she might be alive. I'm fighting back tears as I take a seat beside him, and he puts his arms around me. But the words he says aren't the ones I was expecting.

"Mike's surfaced," he says.

"Is he dead?"

"We should be so lucky."

"Where's he at?"

"Scotland."

The air rushes out of my lungs. Scotland. Interesting. When I thought of him, I still pictured him in Vegas. And if not here, at least still in the United States. I'm delighted he's out of the country, but there's something else Harris isn't telling me.

"What's the rest of it?" I ask.

"We picked up his trail because our international counterparts noted him using his passport."

I wrinkle my forehead. "Was he trying to leave the country?"

He's hesitating, but finally says, "No. He got married."

"Married? To who? Satan?"

His smile is small. "No. Vicki."

ABOUT THE AUTHOR

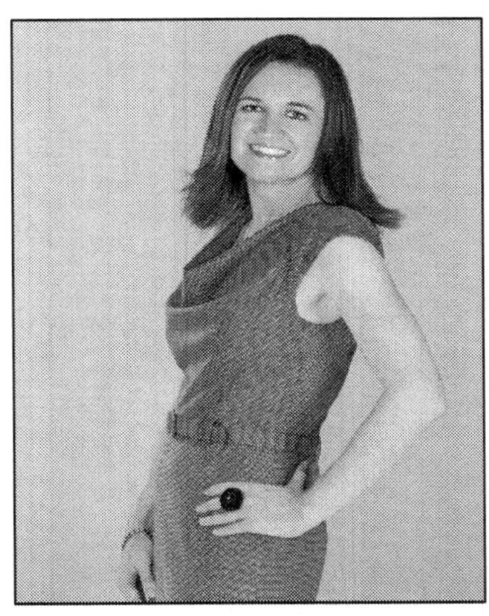

Cat Waters is the pen name for New York Times and USA Today best-selling author Tara Sue Me. Cat lives in the Southeastern United States with her husband, two children, two dogs, and a cat.

www.tarasueme.com

Also by Tara Sue Me

The Submissive

The Dominant

The Training

The Chalet

Seduced by Fire

The Enticement

The Collar

Writing as Cat Waters

Altered Allies: A Short Story

Tara Sue Me as Cat Waters

Made in the USA
Lexington, KY
21 October 2015